David Rees has written many novels, most of them about young people, including *In the Tent*, *The Estuary*, and best-selling *The Milkman's On His Way*. In 1978 his novel *The Exeter Blitz* was awarded the Carnegie Medal, and in 1980 he was the winner of The Other Award for his historical novel, *The Green Bough of Liberty*. *Flux* is his second collection of short stories. The first, *Islands*, was published in 1984 by Knights Press.

FLUX

David Rees

THIRD HOUSE (PUBLISHERS)

First published in 1988 by Third House (Publishers)
35, Brighton Road, London, N16 8EQ

Copyright © David Rees 1988

ISBN 1 870188 03 9

Typeset by Rapid Communications Ltd, WC1X 9NW
Printed by Billing & Sons, Ltd, Worcester

Distributed in the United Kingdom by
Turnaround Distribution Co-op Ltd,
27 Horsell Road, London, N5 1XL

Distributed in the United States of America by
Inland Book Company, 254, Bradley Street,
East Haven, Connecticut 06512, U.S.A.
and
Bookpeople, 2929, Fifth Street, Berkeley, California 94710, U.S.A.

Distributed in Australia by Wild & Woolley Pty Ltd,
16, Darghan Street, Glebe, New South Wales 2007, Australia

Distributed in New Zealand by Benton Ross (Publishers) Ltd,
Unit 2, 46, Parkway Drive, Glenfield, Auckland 9, New Zealand

Two of these stories, *Cousins* and *Worms and Graves and Epitaphs*, originally appeared in *Mister* in 1984; and *Coming to Terms* was published in 1980 in *Remember Last Summer*, a collection of short stories edited by John L. Foster, and is reprinted here by permission of William Heinemann Ltd. All three stories have been substantially revised.

Truth, sir, is a profound sea, and few there be that dare wade deep enough to find out the bottom of it.

– Farquhar, *The Beaux-Stratagem*

For Jimmy Cluff
and Bob Henderson

PERSPECTIVES

1 – COMING TO TERMS

Ben Hazell was in the same class at school, the Lower Sixth. Martin Stokes knew his every gesture and movement by heart, and each time he smiled Martin almost exclaimed out loud that another boy could be so attractive, that his own body could be so clumsy and ugly. In his happier moments he thought of his love for Ben as the old man who burdened Sinbad's back – heavy, not intolerable, almost sewn into his life. At other times he watched himself suffer and loathed what he saw; the weight was so crushing that he longed for the courage to turn on the gas-taps and not strike a match. For there was not the slightest chance of his feelings being returned. Ben would undoubtedly mock and jeer, or react with complete disgust should he ever learn the truth.

Martin had worked out, months ago, which way his beloved came home from school. Ben played games most nights, football practices, putting the shot, or leaping into the long-jump pit. Martin tried to meet him – accidentally on purpose – somewhere along the route.

On the first occasion Ben said, 'Surely you don't live down here? You live next door to Malcolm Price, don't you?'

'It's just as easy this way.' Martin did not dare to look at him.

'Strange. I could have sworn it was longer.' Ben did not really like his company – it was often rumoured that

1

Martin was a pouf – but he was too good-natured to allow this to show. He felt, obscurely, that it was his duty to be kind to those less fortunate than himself.

Martin took to waiting for him in the High Street. The occasions had to be spaced out; if he was there every night Ben would be suspicious. The fifth time they met Ben said, 'Why are you always hanging about here?'

'I like this shop.' It was a junk shop; old chairs and tables were piled up inside so that there was scarcely room to move. But it had a convenient porch for standing in, and the customers were so few that Martin felt he was comparatively unnoticed.

'I sometimes think you wait for me deliberately.'

Martin blushed. 'What . . . do you mean?'

'People at school say you fancy me. I thought it was a joke, but now I wonder. You don't, do you?'

Martin's heart leaped and pounded. 'Yes,' he said.

Ben whistled in surprise. The street lighting made his face seem pale, like a statue. His hair was black and curly, his eyes brown, trusting. 'Is that why you've been dancing attendance on me?' he asked.

'Sssh!' A man went by, and Martin interpreted his stare as meaning that he'd overheard the conversation.

Ben watched him till he had turned the corner, then said, 'You mean you want to have it off with me?' Martin writhed in embarrassment, and walked away. 'Hey! Don't go!'

He waited for Ben to catch him up. He felt sick. His legs were like water.

'Have you done it with other boys?'

'Of course not!' It was a nightmare, this conversation, quite different from anything he had imagined. He was sure Ben would never want to see him again.

'I took it all for a joke.'

'It's not just sex. I love you.'

Ben gazed at him, then burst out laughing. '*Love* me! You *love* me? But I'm not a girl! How can you love me?'

'I just do. Desperately.'

Ben frowned. Martin's intensity disturbed him. 'Don't you try anything,' he said.

2

'Of course I shan't!'

There was a long silence. 'Poor old Marty!' The note of compassion was real. Martin looked up. It was kindness, he saw in a flash, that was Ben's weakness; if he played on that there was hope.

'Can I see you again? Please!' He was a beggar scrabbling for bits of food; *he* could not afford to be generous.

Ben hesitated. 'If it means so much to you I don't mind.' The tone of his voice suggested that he did mind. 'But if the others know I've been walking down dark lanes with you, I'd never hear the end of it!'

It was some time before Martin saw him again, except during school hours. He did not wait at the junk shop every night, but when he did so he was disappointed. Ben must be taking another way home. When they did meet at last, one Saturday lunchtime in King Street, it was by accident.

'Why are you avoiding me?' Martin asked.

The sight of his abject face, his hunched, gangling figure, cowed like a dog, moved Ben. 'It's not intentional,' he said. 'There haven't been any practices this fortnight, so I've been going home early. Tell you what! I'm going to Blaxted Hall tomorrow morning. Do you want to come with me?'

All the rest of the day Martin walked in delight. Perhaps, perhaps Ben felt the same way, just a little; there was no end to the possible happiness tomorrow might bring. He pushed out of his head the voice that told him Ben had only invited him out of pity, and that nothing at all was going to happen.

The Sunday bells woke him. He looked at the blustery day, the jumble of rooftops and chimneys on the hillside. His bedroom window was blurred with the wet of a recent shower; a gale howled round the houses and sang in the telephone wires opposite. Beyond the streets were fields; soon they would both be out there together in the roaring wind, a great skyscape racing overhead.

Blaxted Hall was a millionaire's folly, its style mock Tudor; it had been empty for years. The gardens were overrun with weeds, and the glass in the conservatories had been smashed by vandals. But the mansion itself was still looked after. People came occasionally to clean it and air the furniture in its rooms.

Martin peered into an old wood-warped shed; it was full of rusty garden implements and frayed deckchairs. 'Let's go up to the house,' Ben said. 'We might be able to get inside.'

'How? It's all locked up.'

'Oh . . . ways.' They stopped for a moment by a stable door that was banging in the wind, and Ben closed it.

'You know it well,' Martin said.

'Used to play here as a kid.'

'Why have we come here now?'

'No particular reason. I just thought it might be interesting.'

When they were at the back of the house, Ben said, 'There's a window here that doesn't fit properly.'

Martin listened to the gale tearing headlong through the trees. 'Do you think we should?' he asked.

'Why ever not?' Ben pressed his fingernails under the window-frame and tugged. It swung open. He heaved himself up onto the sill in one easy movement. Martin loved the grace of it; he himself would be certain to fumble when he tried. Ben stood in the kitchen sink, then leaned out of the window, offering his hand. Martin was pulled up as easily as if he were a child. It was a sudden fulfilment of the impossible; he was holding Ben's hand: they were actually touching.

'Thank you,' he said, as Ben let go and jumped down to the floor.

'For holding your hand?' Martin did not answer. 'Don't be so soppy!'

In the drawing room there was wooden linenfold panelling from floor to ceiling. The fireplace was heavy and black, imitation Jacobean. There was a thick carpet and a settee. Upstairs most of the rooms were empty, though some contained beds, wardrobes, chests of drawers. The atmosphere was damp and forlorn; the feeling of neglect that engulfed the whole place was depressing. It was very

4

quiet, totally private. What did Ben want? It was certainly a convenient spot for lovers. Did he. . . ?

But Ben was bored. Now he had shown Martin over the house he kept looking at his watch. 'I must go home soon,' he said. 'Sunday dinner.' They returned to the drawing room, and Martin, wanting to delay things as much as he dared, sat down on a settee. Ben stood by the fireplace, fiddling with a brass poker.

'Does anybody else ever break in here?' Martin said. 'Courting couples?'

'Sometimes.' He looked up. 'I came here once with a girlfriend.'

'Did you?' Silence. 'I didn't know . . . you had a girlfriend.'

'I haven't at the moment.'

'Oh.'

'You're a strange one, Marty. Why don't you . . . get some help?'

'Help? What kind of help?'

'There was something in the *Express and Echo* the other day. My dad was talking about it.' Ben's father was the editor of the local newspaper. 'It caused an argument at the board meeting, apparently; an advertisement for a gay counselling service. Dad thought it should go in and he got his way. He usually does.'

'A gay counselling service? What on earth use would that be to me?'

'Because you're homosexual. And you're very unhappy.'

Martin stared at him. No one had ever spelled it out before in words so specific; he'd not even admitted it to himself quite so baldly. It was true, of course. As true as the fact that he existed, breathed, was standing there. A gay counselling service. He didn't like the idea at all. He didn't want to meet such people; what would they ask of him, what demands would they make? He wouldn't be able to cope. It was safer being isolated, locked up inside himself, loving Ben however unhappy it made him. The thought that somebody else, somebody he didn't find attractive, might want to touch him, was loathsome.

5

'I'm all right as I am,' he said.

Ben shrugged his shoulders. 'Suit yourself. It's your choice.'

'All I want . . . is to see you from time to time. I've enjoyed today.' He had: he had never felt so happy in all his life.

Ben winced. 'Suppose I don't want to see *you*?'

'But . . . but *you* asked *me* to come here, to this house.'

'I felt sorry for you.' Martin didn't answer. He stared miserably at the floor. 'Did you imagine I was going to seduce you or something?' Again, Martin was silent. 'Martin, surely there are others like you. Why don't you seek them out? I'll give you the phone number; I think we've still got the paper at home.' He looked at his watch. 'I must be off; my dinner will be spoiled.'

He kept well out of Martin's way. It was November. The streets were damp with fog and blackened where the swept-up leaves had left a coating of dirt. Martin lingered in the entrance to the junk shop, knowing that to wait in this fog was hopeless, but if he did not he would torture himself all the evening with the thought that Ben might have gone by and he would have missed him. A grey figure loomed out of the night. Martin shrank back into the shop and let him pass, suddenly afraid that Ben might be annoyed at seeing him. He followed, well back, content to walk the same streets, put his fingers on the same railings, or pull at a privet leaf that his beloved had just touched. Ben was a faint wraith in the distance. There was something about the way he moved or turned his head that fascinated: Martin yearned to be him, to be those long legs and arms, that body; only then would he know what was the real worth of being a real person. There was bone, hair, skin, muscle, just as he was, but something else, a mysterious or magical essence that left him a lump of clay in comparison.

He went home, and sat in his room staring at a blank piece of paper. The essay title was *What were the chief results of Palmerston's foreign policy?* He was supposed to hand it in tomorrow, but he could think of nothing to say.

6

Ben flickered in front of his eyes. He slammed his books shut and rushed downstairs. 'I'm going out,' he said to his mother, who looked up from the television and told him not to be late. He decided to walk past the Hazells' house. There was no reason why he shouldn't; it was a free country. They might even speak. The thought of that made him dance inside; his body seemed so buoyant that it was only a husk: everything dull and leaden in him dissolved into light and air. If I don't see him today, he said to himself, I'll come back tomorrow; tomorrow I'll see him. . .

Mrs Hazell was standing at her front door, talking to a friend. Martin's brain snapped a photo of a silver-haired woman in a long dress, wearing pearls: she was the type you met doing refreshments at the school fete or the church bazaar.

Damn anything that happened afterwards: he had to see Ben, had to speak to him. Nothing could be worse than his present suffering.

'Is Ben in, please? I'm . . . er . . . at school with him. I was just passing, and . . . I . . . remembered he lives here.' He was amazed at his own daring: his action was completely impulsive, spur of the moment; if he'd stopped to think he would have gone straight home.

She smiled and held the door open. 'He's upstairs, in his room. You are. . . ?'

'Martin Stokes.'

'Ah.' It meant nothing to her. 'Go on up. There's a lad from school with him anyway. I expect you know him: Malcolm Price.'

'Yes.'

'Straight ahead at the top of the stairs.' Then she shouted, 'Ben! You've got another visitor!'

'Who is it?'

But she had forgotten Martin's name already. 'Go on up,' she said a second time, and resumed her conversation with the woman on the doorstep.

Ben was wearing his school blazer. Malcolm, slim, loose-limbed and blond, an athlete like Ben, was dressed in green corduroy trousers and a leather jacket: he was curled up in an armchair, smoking a cigarette. Turkish:

7

Martin recognized the smell. They were listening to a record, the Electric Light Orchestra. They both stared at him, astonished. 'What the hell are you doing here?' Ben demanded.

'I was passing . . . and . . . I thought I'd just call in.' Martin wished the floor would open and swallow him up. What could have possessed him, driven him to come here? The embarrassment was dreadful.

Games kit lay scattered about the floor – shorts, tee-shirts, plimsolls, two squash racquets. The room was pleasant: a fitted carpet, bookshelves, a gas fire. The armchair in which Malcolm sprawled looked expensive and comfortable.

The music came to an end. Malcolm stubbed out his cigarette. 'I must go,' he said.

'You don't have to,' Ben answered. 'I'll drive you. I can borrow Dad's car.'

'I came on the moped.' He picked up one of the squash racquets. 'I'll leave you both . . . to it.' He winked, and grinned.

'Don't be so bloody stupid!' Ben said angrily, and followed him out of the room.

Martin listened to their conversation as they went downstairs: they were giggling, some huge joke. About him, no doubt. Then Malcolm saying he didn't really think Ben fancied Martin; something like that. He groaned, out loud: why had he come here? He'd ruined it now. Ben would hate him. Why hadn't he done what he'd always done, controlled himself, bottled it up inside? Christ, it was the finish of everything!

They were both drivers, Ben and Malcolm. One more area, Martin thought, which separated him from the others. Ben had been the first of their year to pass the test. It was one of the symbols of male adulthood, like looking down in a lordly fashion from the away-game coach, or telling your mates that a girl last night had let you have the whole lot. 'You're too young to drive,' Mrs Stokes had said on Martin's seventeenth birthday, three months ago. 'I'm not having you careering about the place and getting yourself killed!'

But everyone of his age drove something.

Ben returned. 'Now, listen!' he said, shutting the door behind him and leaning against it as if intruders might batter down his privacy. 'Let's get this straight. This is the first and last time you come barging in here! Whatever must Mal think? You know what a gossip he is! It'll be round the whole school tomorrow that *you* come here in the evenings!'

'I'm sorry.'

'I don't want to see you again. Not in school, nor anywhere else. I don't want to have anything to do with you!'

'Ben . . . please. . .'

'Now just stop it!' He came over and gripped Martin's shoulders. 'Stop it!!' He shook him, hard. Then let go. He sat down in the armchair. 'I'm sorry too,' he said, quietly. 'It shouldn't be like this. But. . .'

'But.'

'Yes. That but. If people thought differently. . .' There was a long silence. 'I found that phone number. Do you want it?'

'What phone number?'

'The counselling service.'

'Oh. Yes, all right.'

Ben gave him a newspaper cutting. 'Clear off now, will you?' he said. 'I've got a mountain of homework to do.'

Martin, in his bedroom, looked at his face in the wardrobe mirror. Christians said God had made man in His image, but, he thought, flawed copies were sometimes pressed as He did so: quirks, cripples, jokers in the pack. God, if there was such a thing as God, must be a humorist. 'Run, you cripple!' he whispered at his reflection. Cripple? Not totally. What had happened at Ben's house had proved that. Ben wasn't perfect; that had been demonstrated very clearly. Martin wouldn't have behaved in the same way if the roles had been reversed, rejecting someone in need just because of what people might think. Ben, of course, had never been in his position: the target of sniggers and silly remarks. It wasn't as hard to put up with as Ben made out. Rejected love was much harder to bear; you were offering another person the most precious of all gifts and it was thrown back in your face. At least in one way he was a better person than Ben. 'Learn to love yourself,' he said to the mirror. Ben certainly loved himself. 'Accept,' he whispered. 'Accept!' Then, perhaps, falling in love wouldn't be confused with a desire to be someone different from what he was himself, wouldn't be tangled up in a chaotic mess with envy and self-hatred.

Ben didn't want to see him. Well . . . he would obey that request, though it was like a prison sentence. But, he was surprised to discover, it was not a death sentence. He felt, for the first time, morally superior. Ben was ordinary, with feet of clay, as he was. 'If people thought differently. . .' What a twisted, devious thing to feel!

But Ben . . . I still love you.

Malcolm had talked. Suddenly everyone at school seemed to know that Martin Stokes was in love with Ben Hazell; he was jeered at more than usual, called all kinds of rude names. But Ben didn't seem to suffer any loss of status. He went around with the same friends, even joined in the laughter. He never spoke to Martin nowadays. The humour was cruel, often obscene. One morning when Martin came into the History class, he saw written on the blackboard in huge white letters the words MARTIN STOKES IS QUEER, and a bleeding heart pierced with an arrow. Inside the heart were the initials B.J.H. He rubbed it out, while the others looked on, grinning.

He was very alone. But his feelings were not quite the same as they had been; how could you really love someone who scorned you, who, deep down, detested you, or at the very least profoundly mistrusted you? The fantasies he had once woven around Ben were so patently absurd that they no longer helped him to get through the days. But his isolation was giving him a kind of strength: he didn't hate himself now.

The slip of paper Ben had given him he'd put away in a drawer at home. Perhaps it would be the best thing to do, the *only* thing to do: dial those figures. No. He didn't want to get mixed up with that. Mixed up with what? He had to admit that he knew nothing about the people represented by that telephone number. There was no good reason to assume they would fill him with horror.

One evening he saw Ben walking up the High Street, his arm round a girl. They didn't look particularly happy together, Martin thought. Ben saw him, but he made no sign of recognition. Next day, at school, Martin met him in the library. There was no one else in there. It was a farce, he thought, this pretence that they didn't even know each other. Why should he let himself be pushed into playing such a ridiculous game? He would speak: to hell with the consequences.

'Hello,' he said.

Ben turned a page, pretending to concentrate fiercely on his book. 'Hello,' he replied, as distantly as he could.

'I saw you last night.'

'Spying as usual, were you?'

Martin paused. 'Why do you have to be so unpleasant?' he asked. Though the reason was obvious: the gossip had made Ben the one who couldn't be generous now.

'I don't like you. I don't want to have anything to do with you. Leave me alone!'

'Afraid you're just a little bit like me? Is that it?' His own voice, for once, had a hint of mockery. Why had he said that? It had come out, quite unthinkingly; he didn't even know if there was the smallest grain of truth in it.

Ben threw the book at him, as hard as he could. It missed. 'I'd sooner be dead than be like you!'

'That's sad.'

'Oh . . . get knotted! Fuck off!' He got up and walked out of the room.

Martin heaved a sigh, then said, 'In the long run it might just conceivably be your loss, not mine.' But Ben was out of earshot.

He opened the phone-box door with beating heart. He'd memorised the number, ages ago. Someone was answering. He put the receiver down and ran into the street. He hadn't thought it out clearly enough, he reasoned; it was an emotional response to what had happened. Not a time for rational decisions.

It's your only hope, he said to himself, your only hope! But what would they want from him, those people on the other end of the phone? Get him in their clutches. What clutches? They were human beings, like him. Like him! It was a woman who had answered: that was a surprise. Dialling that number was a final admission, a final acceptance of knowing he was homosexual. As the Jews had had to sew the star of David onto their clothes. The final solution. If he had been a Jew in Hitler's Germany he might well have been very frightened to wear that star.

It's your only hope. Try it; the dead weight of Ben might drop, like the burden from Sinbad's back, into the sea. Try it. *There's nothing to lose*.

This time he let it ring.

2 – MARJORAM TEA ROOMS

It was a wet and windy day at the end of June when Carl and I went to Norton's bookshop to buy a crib to *Antony and Cleopatra*, the Shakespeare set for our 'A' levels. Our purchase completed, we walked out into a gust of cold rain. A bitter wind funnelled up Waterbeer Street, and blew a lost newspaper against a bus windscreen. The NO WAITING sign groaned in agony; shop blinds slapped like yacht sails. A woman hurried past, tugged along by her umbrella.

'Mal!' Carl shouted. 'Let's go next door!' He wriggled down into his raincoat. 'We can't go home in this.' The rain swept at us, almost horizontally, in stinging grey lines. 'Come on!'

Next door was the Marjoram Tea Rooms; you might find our mothers in there on shopping days, chatting over morning coffee and biscuits. We burst in in a flurry of laughter and cold air and raindrops shaking from our coats.

'Look!' said Carl, after he had ordered two coffees. 'See who's here!' He pointed to the corner beyond the hat-stand, away to his right. Somebody's mother, I thought, but it was Ben and a man I did not recognize. I pushed my chair back and stood up.

'Don't do that!' Carl said. 'Don't let them see us!'

'Why not?'

'Don't you know what Mr Hazell is like? Listen.'

The rain washed the windows and the wind shook them; cars splashed through water in the street and buses were high and straining in third gear on Cornmarket Hill: women's voices bubbled and coffee spoons clinked. Ben's father's words pierced through it all clearly.

'I'm afraid I've found it necessary to upgrade the morning room, Ben.' The voice was high and too cultured. 'You see, I need a sort of place where I can write a few things before lunch and receive people.' Carl was laughing soundlessly. I swivelled, but all I could see was the back of Mr Hazell's neatly brushed greying head and Ben's dark hair. He was already taller than his father. 'I know you like the morning room to sprawl about in, but I thought you might move into the drawing room.'

Ben mumbled something in reply.

'No, I don't mean you sprawl literally, dear boy; I mean you like to leave objects around in there, don't you? Books and sports kit and things. Perhaps the linen room would be better for you, really; Mummy's too terribly busy in the drawing room in the mornings tidying up. We'll move the linen out, of course; I don't know . . . but . . . we'll find somewhere; Packard won't object . . . of course, I have it! My study! I mean, if I'm moving into the morning room, I shan't want . . . shall I?'

Mumble mumble mumble.

'Ben, you mustn't be unreasonable about it. It really means upgrading the linen room too if you're moving in. We shan't call it the linen room, naturally; we'll call it . . . ah . . . er . . . the den.'

Mumble mumble.

'But Mummy would be so frightfully cross without the drawing room! It's sort of not quite really hers anyway with the television being in there. I don't see how we could give her a proper boudoir upstairs; there isn't room. No, it's a frightful problem, but I think I've hit on the best solution.'

Mumble mumble mumble mumble mumble mumble.

'You don't seem to be able to appreciate my point of view, Ben. I've got Roger and Delia and the other Roger dropping in every day now, and sometimes Penny comes too. I must have *room*, Ben. One simply can't breathe in that poky little study. I asphyxiate! It's really too *awful* for words!'

Carl choked into his coffee, causing it to spill into the cake-dish. A meringue was saturated.

Suddenly the room was filled with light. The rain had stopped; the sun was transforming the shop-front opposite into a glaring oblong of brilliance and a parked van's outline became a long dazzling streak. The edge of the kerb glittered like gold icing. As we looked the Hazells passed us and went out into the sunshine. Ben must have seen us but he gazed stonily ahead.

'There's Anna,' Carl said, getting up hurriedly. 'Come on.'

'We don't want to catch up with the Hazells, do we?'

'She was going the other way.'

I paid the bill. The waitress was slow and Carl began to fidget.

'Who's Anna?' I asked, very casually, as if I didn't care anything about the details of my friend's private life.

'Oh . . . just a girl. Come on.'

So, I thought. And Ben, of course, had been going out with girls ever since the Second Form. Once more I felt a chill of irritation. I was being left behind in the race.

Outside I let Carl go. The wind pushed him after the girl, who was now a distant flutter of pink. Martin Stokes was walking down the other side of the street, with a man. Martin was a pouf. It made me uneasy when I thought of it: someone like that living in the house next door; well, it couldn't bode any of us any good. I turned away from them into the wind.

14

On the bus home I thought about Ben and his father. My crib to *Antony and Cleopatra* lay unopened on the seat beside me; the very idea of it was boring in the extreme. I arrived home feeling inexplicably depressed. Life, I was sure, was passing me by.

3 – SUMMER DARK

Aged eighteen and the end of the summer term, the last day of the school year: it was the last day of all for most of us, though not for me and Ben – we were to return in September to sit for Cambridge scholarships at Christmas. It was a silly, emotional day, and I longed for it to be over, for I throbbed with anticipation each time I thought of the evening: John Hallett was celebrating his release by throwing a party, and I was taking the first girl I had ever fallen for – deeply, that is. Tonight I knew would be a landmark in my life; our talk and laughter was bound to become magic with the hot summer night, the music, the dancing on the lawn, the drink; there would be friends of ours there, other lovers: making love perhaps. I was to take the car, for the party would end long after my parents were in bed. It was not the first time I had been allowed the car at night without adult supervision; but it was still a rare enough privilege for me to find the prospect exciting.

'Be careful,' my mother said, as I waved goodbye.

'I will,' I promised, and I set off, in my imagination swirling down country lanes with Anna in the summer night after the party. I drew up outside her house exactly on time. She came down the stairs, the excitement of a special occasion evident in her blush and dancing eyes and the anxious look that said, 'Am I all right?' The sea-blue dress left her arms and neck bare; it rustled on the clothes underneath. She wore no make-up, and this I took as a good omen; she knew how much I disliked make-up, but this was the first time for ages she had worn none.

15

Mr Barker came into the hall to tell us not to be too late home.

'How late's too late, Dad?'

'Well . . . it's not that I fuss, of course . . . but it's your mother.' He coughed loudly. 'She worries, you know, and she won't sleep till you're in.'

'She usually taps on the bedroom wall, even that time I wasn't back till one.'

'Hmmm. Well . . . enjoy yourselves. Don't stand about on the doorstep when you come home; that wakes *me* up.' He coughed again, and shuffled back to the TV programme he and his wife were watching.

'How embarrassing parents are,' Anna said, 'particularly when they think they are modern and liberal.' Are they, I thought, and wondered at what point their liberalism stopped.

Although we were not very late we were nearly the last to arrive. People had sensed, apparently, that this was going to be a good party, and they had come on time. John met us at the door with 'It's Anna and Mal!' and I heard someone inside repeat it, and then 'Animal!', a stupidity I had by now almost got used to. Claire, John's girlfriend, ushered Anna upstairs for coats and mirrors and gossip; I stayed with John in the hall. I had known him since we were six; we had been in the same form through two schools, a period of twelve years, but during all that time the number of occasions we had been alone together, talking, could not have been more than half a dozen. As I looked at his face, I knew that the face I gave him in the rare moments I thought of him was completely inaccurate; while I was growing up I had forgotten, somehow, that he too was growing up, and that the child who was lost in me was just as lost in him. For a moment or two, the John who stood there, who was my age and whose face was dark from shaving, surprised me by existing at all.

The girls came down, laughing and chatting much more easily than we were.

'John's parents have been super,' Claire said. 'There's heaps of food and they've been terribly generous with the drink.' I had met Claire before, and though she was

16

very tennis-club I liked her. John, I considered, was a bit dour for her, and another piece of the past came to me as I remembered how different he was years ago, the ringleader of mischief and merriment at our primary school.

'My parents have gone out,' he said. 'Thank God! At first they weren't going to. Can you imagine? Then there was some office function Dad decided they shouldn't miss. But fancy suggesting they'd stay! Would yours have done?' It was the longest speech he'd made to me in years.

I didn't like to admit that my parents would certainly not have allowed a teenage party to go on at all, unsupervised, till the small hours. 'They'd clear off,' I said. 'No problem.'

Claire looked impressed. 'Mine are so old-fashioned,' she said. 'They think everyone's going to leap into bed as soon as their backs are turned. You're lucky.'

In the front room the carpet had been taken up, the furniture removed, and six or seven couples were dancing. The records were hits of years ago, Abba, Stars on Forty-five, the Beatles. Barry Robson was sitting on the floor; he was alone and seemed very unhappy. I felt sorry for him, and smugly superior. Parties made me unsure of myself, conscious of the precarious foothold in this society that I clung to. Others probably felt the same; when we paraded our best clothes or our girlfriends, we knew we were building defences or hurling defiances at the boys we had known all our lives. Carl was talking to a girl I had not seen before. I was surprised; what had happened to Barbara? There was evidently some gossip I had missed. He waved, but it was not a wave that said, 'Come and join us.'

I turned to John. 'What have you done with the carpet?' I asked.

'It's in the garage with the furniture,' Claire said. She flashed me a radiant smile, and though there was no one else I could conceivably want to hold in my arms than Anna, it gave my wilting confidence a boost. Then Anna moved her cheek against mine, and I bent down to kiss her. As we drew apart, I found myself in Carl's level gaze; but he returned at once to his conversation with the girl.

Later, as we went into the dining room for supper, I said to myself that whatever magic fulfilment was to happen this evening had certainly not happened yet. We helped ourselves to food; quiches and salad, bread and paté, pineapple and cheese wedged on sticks, little bits of toast covered in dark substances with piercing tastes. We stood by the open French windows and talked to Kevin about a lurid sex film that had recently been in town. We had all seen it; we all had to see it: it was the subject of several angry letters to Mr Hazell's paper. After the film, as I kissed Anna, she did not say as the heroine had said, 'When are you going to screw me again?' She had not enjoyed the evening; as we came out of the cinema she said she had been bored. Bored!

We talked for a long time with Kevin, almost spinning the conversation out needlessly. Perhaps we were frightened of taking the plunge into the darkening garden (Kevin would obviously not come too); to show the depths of my feelings to Anna seemed now more like an ordeal than a moment of magic. How much did I love her anyway? Wasn't all this high-minded emotion really hypocrisy? Wasn't it sex I wanted, and, equally important, to let my friends know I was having it? Better not be humiliated by a rebuff; stay here and talk to Kevin.

'You know who that is with Ben?' he said. She had frizzy blonde hair and wore a vivid scarlet dress; her face was angular and unattractive. There was almost no gap between her nose and her upper lip. 'That's the famous Zoe!' He laughed.

'Is it?' I looked at her with new eyes. Ben was the only one of us who was having a successful, long-term, sexual relationship. He had always ventured on things before we did; his third date with Zoe, Kevin informed me, had been in her bed. As I looked at her I was surprised there was no branding mark on her that pronounced that she was no longer virgin; she looked perfectly ordinary – ugly even.

'Let's go into the garden,' I said to Anna, and Kevin went off to talk to Barry Robson.

It was still light, but the bushes and trees were black against the sky. Flowers were already difficult to distinguish, but scents – summer jasmine, roses, honeysuckle, tobacco plants – were heady and exotic, reminders of the elusive magic. Neither of us spoke. The garden was huge; at the end of the lawn the trees began, so many of them it was almost a wood. I heard someone laugh, and saw the glow of a cigarette. It was too dark to make out who it was. Then I heard Carl's voice: 'But if you hadn't done so then, you would have sooner or later. The main thing is you came to that match and I didn't have to bat.' Then her voice murmured, like the bubbles of a stream, but I could not hear the words. Anna pulled at my sleeve, and I realised we were standing still in order to listen. I was hurt. It was Carl, more than any of my friends, in whom I confided, and he never stopped telling me – or so I thought – what he was up to. But this girl, whoever she was, he had kept a close secret.

Five minutes later Anna said, 'You're very quiet.' She had ceased to exist while I fumed against Carl. We were standing by the edge of a pond at the side of the garden. The party and the house were a long way away – squares of light from windows, for the curtains had not been drawn. Irene Carra singing *Fame* drifted to us on the night air.

We did not talk for some while. Kissing was enough. Then, increasingly, it was not enough, though I pressed my tongue through the oval of her mouth, and she responded, hers exploring mine. My hand was on her leg, and I gently moved it up. She shifted away from me.

She said: 'I keep teeth in there. They'll bite you.' We were separate now, not touching at all.

'Will they bite it right off?'

'Yes, so don't try.'

Silence. Then I said, nervously, 'I'd like to try.' There was no answer. 'Please.' Still no answer. 'I love you,' I said. 'I want to make love.' And I added, grotesquely, 'I'd like to marry you.'

'Don't be daft.'

'It's true.'

19

She giggled. 'You're still at school,' she said. And *she* wasn't; she was that much more adult, even if she was only a junior assistant in the public library. I took her in my arms again, but there was no response now; her kisses were flat.

'I love you,' I whispered as I kissed her on both eyes. 'Let's make love. Let's make love!'

'We can't. Certainly not here.'

'You mean . . . somewhere else?'

'No, no, I don't.'

'What then?'

'I'm not . . . going to. . .'

'Why not?'

'Why not? Because I'm just . . . not. Don't pester me.'

'Don't you love me at all?'

'Yes. No. I don't know. Don't keep pushing me; I'm so confused!'

'Why do you come out with me, then? You just want a good time; that's it, isn't it?'

'Of course not! Do have some sense. I can't just say, like that, I'll sleep with you! You're not thinking about me at all.'

'I just want us to be completely happy.'

'No!!' She moved away a few steps. Then stopped, a dim blue shape against the trees. I stayed where I was, small and ashamed. Tonight had been ripped in tatters. It was no landmark in my life.

'Don't sulk,' she said. 'Let's go indoors.'

'You go,' I replied. 'I'll stay out here for a bit.' She did not need a second invitation.

I was tempted to walk out of the garden and go home. But I couldn't possibly allow my friends to see that my love-life was ruined; I would have to look as if everything was wonderful, right to the bitter end of the party. I leaned against a tree and lit a cigarette. I'd go into the house in a moment.

There was someone – two people – in the darkness, not far away. I turned my back on them, deciding to follow Anna; then stopped. There was something strange about this couple. I peered into the gloom: two faces were

20

kissing. Then, a pair of hands was unbuttoning a shirt. Locked in a tight embrace, both bodies slowly subsided onto the ground, and I could see no more.

Jeans unzipping. Mouths. Breath.

The two bodies were male. The one whose hands were unbuttoning the shirt I had never seen before; but the other – Martin Stokes. What on earth was *he* doing here? John Hallett would never have invited *him*! Not in a thousand years!

I was shocked. Appalled. Disgusted? I was surprised to find I was not disgusted. And – very much against my will – I discovered I was erect.

Maybe I should go indoors immediately, I said to myself. It would probably go down before I rejoined the party; no one would notice anything amiss. But . . . I didn't move.

Some time later I heard the two bodies gasp.

From the side of the garage came a violent choking. I saw a man sway against a trellis. Then came the same sound; his whole body shuddered, and he spilled sick onto the flowers. There was an overpowering smell of beer. Barry Robson. I tried to hold him upright, and where my hand gripped his jacket there was slime. He tottered like an unstable sack.

'I'm O.K.,' he grunted. His stomach churned again; he retched, but there was nothing more to bring up. 'Leave me alone.'

I pulled him towards the house; he was suddenly as pliant as a child. His mouth gaped open and shut, and long strings of saliva trickled down his suit. The voice of Edith Piaf came from the record player –

> Quand il me prend dans ses bras
> Il me parle tout bas,
> Je voie la vie en rose. . .

I opened the door, and the sound was suddenly amplified; music, talk, laughter from the next room.

There was nobody in the kitchen. On the draining boards and table, the cooker, every available surface,

21

were piles of dirty crocks – plates with crumbs, fruit bowls with smears of trifle on the sides where spoons had scraped, cups with lipstick smudges and little dried ladders of coffee grouts. I flopped Barry into a chair. His legs sprawled out in front of him, and his arms and head hung as if they were too heavy for him. His face had the look of candle grease and when I touched it his skin was hot and tacky. The smell of sick reminded me of babies.

''S all very well for you,' he muttered. 'You're all right.' I did not reply, and he said, 'Was no girl here for Barry. Chriss, I feel weak.'

'I think I'd better take you home.'

'No. I'llbeallrightinaminute,' he slurred, and pulled at his tie. I undid the top buttons of his shirt and his head fell forwards. His long hair hung down in front of him, and I thought of a plant trailing over the side of a flower-pot. There was an opened bottle of wine on the table. I picked it up and drank straight from it. When I put it down it was a third gone.

'You zhrank zhat like fucking orangeade,' Barry said, grinning.

'I'm going to take you home,' I repeated, staggering slightly as the effect of the wine percolated into my knee-caps and leg bones.

'Dondozhat, Malcolm,' he pleaded. 'Zhere's some fab-u-lous birds here. I'm gonnascrewsome . . . screw . . . some. . .'

The outside door opened, and Martin came in with the stranger. I *had* seen this man before. He had been walking down the street with Martin the day Carl and I bought our cribs to *Antony and Cleopatra*. I stared at them, coldly. Martin stared back: his eyes were shining. He looked deliriously happy.

'I'm Ian, John's brother,' the stranger said. 'This is my friend, Martin. Do you know him? You probably go to the same school.'

'I know him,' I said, sourly.

Ian Hallett. I was vaguely aware of his existence, but I had never met him. An older, more attractive version of John; aged perhaps twenty-five. The only thing I knew about him was that he worked for Ben's father on the local paper.

'John told me to bring a friend to this bash,' Ian said. 'So who better than Martin?' They smiled at each other.

A long silence. 'Let's go into the dining room,' he said. 'See if there's anything the vultures haven't eaten.'

As they left, his fingers briefly touched Martin's face.

John, when I found him, was looking worried. 'Everyone's going to the bedrooms!' he said, dramatically.

'Everyone?' The room was packed with dancers; the hall was full of people drinking, and couples lay entwined on the stairs. Ben was talking to Zoe, the very picture of respectability. They were eating cold sausages.

'Someone's in my parents' bedroom and the door's locked!' We looked at each other, both of us evidently struck by the same thought: anywhere else wouldn't matter. One's parents' bedroom – it was as taboo as incest. For a moment I had the same feelings I'd experienced in the garden: shock, then desire.

'Surely they could have gone into your room,' I said.

'Carl's in there screwing Vanessa. I went in to fetch a handkerchief and switched on the light; it was most embarrassing!'

'Is that really her name?'

'Vanessa? Yes.' Screwing. I had a sudden vision of a Christmas card, to be sent to me in years to come, a snow scene from that ageing couple, the old friend and his wife with the unusual name: 'From Carl, Vanessa and the children.' John puffed at a cigarette. 'What the hell am I going to do if my parents come home early?'

'I'll take somebody off your hands,' I said. 'Barry's in the kitchen, legless. I'll drive him home, then come back for Anna.'

'You're a real friend,' John said, gratefully.

Barry's eyes were shut; his head lolled, and his breathing was loud and heavy. John dragged him to his feet and we wrapped his arms round our necks. For a moment we were motionless, three clowns about to tumble; then we walked him unsteadily out to the car.

I had the engine started when I remembered that I didn't know where he lived; I had to go back indoors to get the address from John. Barry had been to my house often enough, but few of us had ever been to his. He lived in a poor part of town and his father was a shop assistant – that much we all knew; only John knew more. Barry obviously felt ashamed of his background; most of us grammar school boys came from the big housing estates built in the sixties and seventies, but he did not. It was stupid, I thought; after all, my father was only an ordinary office-worker.

Barry was in no state, however, to worry about who was penetrating his home defences; he was fast asleep. His house was in darkness. I fumbled in his pockets and found a bunch of keys. Coming that close to him gave me a feeling of sickness; his breath still stank of beer, and the vomit on his lapels was barely dry. I managed to select the right key and haul him inside. The problem was to get him upstairs – he was a dead, helpless weight – and into his room without disturbing his parents. I might be blamed, being the nearest person at hand, for causing their son's condition. I shook him hard and, for a second, he opened his eyes. Then he fell, heavily. I went into the kitchen, looking for water, certain that his parents would soon be on the scene. But when I returned he was still lying on the floor, and no one had appeared. I splashed the cup of water into his face and he woke and blinked, amazed. Water ran from his nose and chin. I pointed to the stairs and he crawled up to his room; then sank down on the bed and went to sleep immediately.

It didn't seem right to let his mother find him like that in the morning, so I decided to undress him. Only once did he surface towards consciousness: as I pulled off his trousers he murmured, 'Donremovemyknickers.' His body was as pale as his face and he was so still he looked like a wax figure, a Madam Tussaud's dummy. He seemed very young, almost angelic; I looked older and more hard-bitten, I thought. I pushed the quilt over him and left, thinking it wasn't a boy I had hoped to undress that evening. Or – yet another shock – *was* it a boy? In the

24

garden, I had wanted Ian's hands, or Martin's hands, or both their hands, on my prick. *Anybody's* hands other than my own. But my own it had been. I wanted to climb into bed with Barry. Remove his knickers.

I pushed these appalling thoughts out of my mind.

The night was cooler; parked cars glistened with dew. On the drive back I switched on the heater and it purred its warmth round me like a cosy rug. It must have been nearer one than midnight. The houses I passed were shut to the world, curtains drawn and lights out. I pictured the front bedrooms of the pairs of semis – I was through the town centre now and heading up the London Road – each with its dressing table in the bay, double bed for Mum and Dad (it was a middle-aged sort of area), headboard against the boxroom wall: their lives exactly mirrored in the next-door house. On Ipswich Hill I stopped the car and looked back. Buildings were dim like dream-shapes, indistinguishable from one another; only the street lamps, marking the town's veins, stood out, brilliant orange globes and tiny yellow pinpricks. Overhead, as if through a million holes in a gorgeous blue-black cloth, the stars clustered so thickly they could almost be jostling each other for room, and they too, like the street lamps, glittered, so that everywhere, above and below, shining eyes looked at me. From gardens drifted the scents: jasmine, roses, honeysuckle, tobacco plants. Take now, everything said; take now, or it will be too late: don't waste being young and in love.

Martin wasn't wasting it.

When I returned to the Halletts' there was still a couple languidly smooching to the record player, and a few indefatigable eaters in the dining room chewing the last bits of quiche. In the hall there was a smashed glass and spilled red wine, then on the stairs two shapes I recognized. I kicked noisily on the bottom step and John unwound from Claire.

'You've been ages,' he said, stifling a yawn.

'I had to undress him. Where's Anna?'

'Gone.'

'Gone! Where? I mean. . .'

25

'Several of them went off in Kevin's car. Anna said it was so late, and you were so long, she. . .' He petered out, uncomfortable from my gaze, then his shoulders moved with a slight shrug. It wasn't his fault; it wasn't his business.

'I'd best be going then,' I said. 'It's been a great party.'

'Cheers, Mal. Thanks for looking after Barry.'

Claire smiled sleepily. Before I got to the kitchen door they were in each other's arms again. The bottle of wine was where I had left it. I took another long swig; I would have drunk it all had it not snorted back into my nose and made me splutter.

Wild, melodramatic ideas came into my head. I would drive round to her house, bang loudly on the door and demand an explanation. Create a huge scene. But my only untypical action was to light a new cigarette from the butt of the old one. It didn't matter if I died from lung cancer: life had passed me by.

It hadn't passed me by, of course. Six months later, I met a girl at a Christmas party and took her to bed that same night. The following day, my nineteenth birthday, I heard that I'd won a scholarship to Cambridge.

Just prior to these events, Martin Stokes told me the places where I could find men. So I'm beginning to explore both worlds.

Martin, a great guy, is now one of my closest friends.

WATSONVILLE

Stephen Agate, my other half, had been in London on business most of the week; when he came home he was too worn out to make proper, passionate love. But not so worn out, he said, that he didn't want something – he hadn't seen my flesh for five days. He ought to be fed up with it by now, and I with his. We've been lovers for thirty years – we first had sex when we were seventeen – and in all that time we haven't got tired of one another in bed. For this, I think, we should be in the Guinness Book of Records, along with the landlady of our local pub who *is* in it. (She's failed the driving test more times than anybody else in the world.) So we took off our clothes, lay side by side between the sheets, and played with each other's cocks. I like doing this: it puts me in touch with the adolescent I once was. Two kids, wanking. I have to admit that in those days I was always trying to persuade Stephen to progress to more sophisticated pastimes, but he was worried about this; scared it would be painful, even cause him some kind of permanent damage. He consulted a book he found in, of all unlikely places, the public library. 'You would have to use a lubricant,' he said. 'And I don't think you've got the nerve to go into a chemist's and ask for it.' He had underestimated me, however. I went into Boots the very next day and spent a whole week's pocket money on a tube of jelly.

The exquisite sensations that stuff gave us both! And

still does. (Not, I hasten to add, the same tube.) The juice of life, I call it. My body has changed out of all recognition, of course, since we were two teenagers lying on a bed, experimenting with our first lubricant. I didn't have this gone-to-seed weight-lifter's build; the sagging tits, the chest hair, the fattening stomach, the flabby arm muscles. I was slim, trim, and wiry. But Stephen says I'm more attractive now than I was then, and, to my perpetual astonishment, he seems to mean it. He hasn't changed as much as I have, though his face is lined now. His blond hair is thinner, but it continues to stick up so that he looks like a man in a cartoon who's just had a massive electric shock: it was this extraordinary hair, I remember, that made me want him in the first place. But he hasn't become obese, despite gorging himself on incredible quantities of all the wrong foods. His body is still as it was. I love it, him, as much, no, even more now than I did then.

I'd fancied him for nearly three months, but I didn't dare to do anything about it. Well, how could I know what his reaction to such a piece of news would be? He might have run a mile. One afternoon, at the end of a particularly hectic, animal football game, I limped off the field into the school's changing-rooms, covered from head to foot in mud and blood, stripped off all my clothes, then found every shower was occupied. I pulled the curtain of the first one open, and . . . there he was. 'Hurry up, Agate,' I said. 'My need is greater than yours.'

'But I've only just got in here!' he protested.

'If you don't come out, I'll drag you out. I'm bigger and stronger than you are.'

'Why don't we share it?'

Why not, indeed? Standing in that tiny space, our bodies unavoidably touching, I was within seconds as rigid as a flagpole. So, I observed to my delight, was he. Only a few more seconds and our hands were busy; but it was much too quick, the strength of the sex drive at seventeen being what it is. The hot water washed it off, and, mingled together, it swirled down the drain. As we got dressed, we grinned at each other shyly, but our eyes were dancing.

28

He said, eventually, 'You don't live far away from me.' (Three streets off; I had made a point of checking this information. I had walked past his house four or five times in the hope that he would be in the garden, or looking out of a window, and I could therefore get into a conversation with him. But he was never there when I went by.) 'Come home with me,' he suggested. 'My parents are out.'

'O.K.,' I said. Nonchalantly.

A great deal of kissing this second time, and exploring of bodies. Then, lying side by side on his bed, we did it just as we were doing it now, thirty years later. He said, 'I've been after you for weeks. I'm in love with you.'

God! How lucky we've been compared with most men and women! We've never, either of us, fallen for anybody else, though in our twenties we slept with other people. We've never wanted to split up, and no one has tried to part us. Our families, when we plucked up courage to tell them, said they'd guessed, and if we were happy then so were they. We went on to study at the same university, and shared rooms there; then both of us followed reasonably successful careers as journalists. We've travelled the world. Been fulfilled. The only problem is, when one of us dies what will happen to the one who is left? We are inseparable. Symbiotic. I cannot imagine existence without Stephen; if he died, I don't know what I'd do.

All these thoughts and more were going through my mind as we made love. It takes time now, time enough for plenty of thoughts; we can't, nor do we want to, rush to orgasm in seconds. But I was certainly enjoying it, and the reminders of past pleasures. I remembered something else: while Stephen was away, I had been sorting out the attic of our house – tidying up thirty years' accumulated junk. 'On Tuesday I found Watsonville's famous black book,' I said.

'Whose famous black book?'

'Don't tell me you've forgotten!' (It was at the centre of one of the most extraordinary episodes of our school life.)

'Alan . . . I think I'm coming!' He writhed and flopped his head about, moaning and panting, just as he had done during that initiation in the shower; and it turned me on as it had done then, as it always did. My orgasm was not long in following.

'Watsonville,' I said, as I wiped our skins with a towel.

'Watsonville? I thought it was a city in California. Near Soledad. Didn't we drive through it once? We were covering an earthquake.'

'You obviously don't remember. We had this daft trick at school, for a brief while, of adding "ville" to our surnames. And prefixing them with "Harry." Don't ask me why; I never knew the reason.'

'Eric Watson!' he exclaimed.

'Yes. Eric Watson. Except we called him Harry Watsonville. You were Harry Agateville. I was Harry Nancekie-vill-ville. Well . . . I can't help my Cornish surname, can I? That "vill-ville" used to make all the kids bend over double with laughter. Then there was John Barraclough. We christened him Harry Black Barrersville. Because he was black. Beyond Belief Barraclough.'

'It sounds *incredibly* childish.'

'It was,' I said. 'So we soon abandoned the idea. The one name that stuck was Watson's. We *always* called him Watsonville.'

'And you found his famous book?'

'You *must* remember it!'

'Oh, I do. But I didn't know it was in our possession.' The significance of this only now dawned on him. He sat bolt upright. 'It's in *our* possession?'

'Stephen, I'd like to say you're hopeless. That your memory is utterly defective. That you've probably even forgotten our first time in the shower.'

'Don't be ridiculous! It was . . . I guess . . . more important than Watson's black book. Well . . . it seems to have been.' He laughed – nervously, I thought. 'I'll say anything for the sake of a quiet life. Where is it?'

'On the bedside table, right next to you. I stole it.'

'*You* stole it?'

'Yes. It's a secret I've been keeping from you for thirty years.'

'Good God.' He yawned. 'I'm tired. Let's talk about it tomorrow. O.K.?'

30

'Sure.' What an *actor* he is! What a *hypocrite*!

Watsonville – not to put too fine a point on it – was a prostitute, though after he left school he gave up being a player to become a manager: he is a very successful pimp. When I last heard of him, some ten years ago, he was living in the lap of luxury with a wife and three children in the south of France, the source of his wealth being a string of brothels he owned along the whole length of the coast from Menton to Perpignan. My informant also told me that Watsonville's hands now dripped with gold rings, that he owned four Rolls Royces, and that life's fleshpots had made him fatter than King Farouk. The wages of sin, I suppose.

Our educational establishment was a well-known boys' public school of high academic excellence, located in an ultra-salubrious south London suburb. We were mostly day-boys, though there were a few boarders, earnest, hearty, rugger-playing Christians with ya-ya voices and ho-ho laughs. They tended to be somewhat aloof and looked down their noses at us day-bugs; 'You can tell *them* by their *ghastly* accents,' one thin, chinless would-be aristocrat was heard to observe. Presumably they had a sex life in the boarding house: there was an occasional rumour of this or that romance; or A was screwing B, and C was jealous. They had, however, nothing to do with Watsonville, who was, to them, socially quite unacceptable: Australian, flamboyant, indiscreet, and the son of an estate agent. When they knew what Eric was up to, they elevated this snobbish objection to the plane of moral disapproval, though the oldest profession is surely not one that is always outside the provinces of the upper class.

Supervision of the pupils' behaviour at our school was often extraordinarily lax. One of the reasons why Stephen and I enjoyed ourselves so uninhibitedly in the shower was that we knew there was no likelihood of being caught; our games teachers rarely, if ever, bothered to venture into the boys' changing-rooms. They had their own facilities, and a little cubby-hole of an office where

31

sports equipment and lost articles were kept; in there they puffed cigarettes and brewed tea. The same lack of security operated in the cloakrooms. The biggest of these was a huge basement without windows, lit by dim forty-watt lightbulbs; here boys hung up their overcoats in the mornings, and removed them in the evenings. It was never locked, yet I cannot recall any incident of theft; maybe, because it was known to be open all day, people did not leave valuables there. It had little nooks and crannies where the light from the bulbs did not penetrate, and in one of these corners Watsonville conducted his one-man prostitution service.

He would go down there every lunchtime, and wait for his clients. These were vetted and passed on by his henchman, Adrian Muckley, a lewd, filthy-minded fellow, whom Stephen and I found so unacceptably coarse that we didn't speak to him, other than to say 'Hallo' as we passed in the corridors. Unacceptably coarse: that makes us snobbish too. Adrian did have one redeeming feature – or was it? – an overwhelming passion for Wagner. By the age of seventeen he had sat through almost every opera Wagner wrote, including the whole of *The Ring*, which, I said to Agate when I heard, was not so much a pleasure as a masochistic endurance test of extreme severity.

There was no shortage of boys who, at one time or another, went down to the basement for a lunch-hour session with Watsonville. Sitting on a bench in the dark, he manipulated or sucked cock to the point of orgasm and beyond. Two shillings and sixpence was the recognized fee; though it was whispered that a favourite client could get it cut-price or even for nothing, and that particularly unappetising specimens had to pay double, perhaps even treble, the going rate. I think Stephen and I were the only boys in our class – except for boarders and Christians – who voiced disapproval. We found the whole thing tasteless. Not beautiful. But it was easy for him and me to raise aesthetic objections; we were lovers. To love and to be loved means you can *afford* to have aesthetic objections. But it amuses me to look back now and realise that all those customers of Watsonville's were heterosexual: randy boys who didn't yet have girlfriends, or who, if they did, hadn't been allowed more than a few goodnight kisses. Stephen and I were the only gays (not that we knew that at the time, nor, given the date, the nineteen fifties, knew that word.) A nice irony. Yes, all those kids, as far as I know, got married. Some of them will be grandfathers by now. Even Muckley got married: to a German fraulein he met at Bayreuth, a woman of positively operatic shape, truly Wagnerian in dimensions.

Eric, even as a teenager, was a firm believer in correct book-keeping. (He got excellent grades in Mathematics and Advanced Mathematics at 'O' level.) In a notebook with stiff black covers he kept his accounts. Apart from Muckley, nobody knew this – it was a very well-kept secret – but one afternoon, during a French lesson, the entire class got to hear of it.

Our French teacher was an entertaining but inefficient idiot in his early forties nicknamed Hippo. It was a wonderfully apt baptism: he was vast in girth, shambling and lazy, with a long snout-like face and small piggy eyes that appeared to sit right in the top of his head. When he had sunk – immovably, it would seem – into his chair, he looked exactly like an African river-horse; the only things missing were the small birds you see in photographs perched on the backs of hippopotamuses as they joyfully wallow in muddy swamps. He could, however, haul himself out of the chair with surprising speed, usually to go to the lavatory, knocking one of its arms off as he did so – it had been loose for years, and, despite his complaints to the schoolkeeper, it had never been mended. Sometimes, as it fell off, he would quietly say 'Fuck.' Not quietly enough, however; the boys at the front of the class would hear, and burble hysterically. These trips out of the room were frequent during lessons immediately after lunch; Hippo's food was on most days liquid – pints of bitter consumed in the nearest pub, the Cow and Calf. He had been an intelligence officer in the Far East during the War; the Japanese had imprisoned and tortured him, so he said, and he had contracted malaria.

This illness, it was rumoured, wrecked his liver, kidneys and bladder; hence the speed of his excursions to the toilet. Sometimes he forgot to do up his buttons, and, only realising this when he had sat down again in his chair, he would cover himself with one of the volumes of Harrap's Standard French Dictionary and fiddle with his flies. This, inevitably, produced more hysterical twitterings from the boys at the front of the class.

We didn't learn any French from him. In our second year in the Sixth Form we were taught by a brutal, gimlet-eyed, humourless Scotsman who made us work like slaves. Though we didn't appreciate this at all at the time, it was undoubtedly good for us – we mostly succeeded in passing 'A' level French. Two years of Hippo and nobody would have passed. But he was a great talker, regaling us with anecdotes about all kinds of famous people – Evelyn Waugh, the Duchess of Kent, Ava Gardner, Picasso and Stalin, to name but a few – he said he had met in various parts of Planet Earth. (We didn't believe he'd met any of them, of course.) The boys at the front listened; the boys at the back chatted to each other. Hippo didn't care. Until one afternoon, when, the noise level having increased to the point of irritating him, he broke off his monologue, looked up, and said, 'I will *not* tolerate this racket! Watson, what are you doing?'

'Nothing, sir.' (Eric always sat in the back row, next to Muckley.)

'Corrupting Muckley, I imagine. If such a thing is possible, which I doubt.' We all sniggered dutifully. 'What's that book you've got there?'

'Oh . . . er . . . nothing.' It was the accounts book; Eric and Adrian had been taking advantage of Hippo's easy-going discipline to tot up the lunchtime takings. Eric quickly shoved the book into his satchel, which was an extremely foolish thing to do: it aroused Hippo's curiosity.

'Bring it here.'

'What?' Eric looked horrified.

'I said bring it here!' Hippo was beginning to enjoy himself; Watson was evidently up to something rather more interesting than just talking to Muckley. He patted his gigantic stomach, and his piggy eyes became slits. 'Do as you're told, boy!'

'Me . . . sir?'

Hippo began to get cross. 'How many Watsons do you think there are in this room? Bring that book out here at once!' He banged the loose chair arm; it fell off, and, as usual, he said 'Fuck.'

Watsonville had gone so ashen I thought he was going to faint. His mouth, like a fish's, opened and closed, but no words came out. Muckley, too, was white with shock. Eventually Eric was able to utter a few sounds. 'I . . . I . . . think. . .'

'You have one last chance,' Hippo said, as he slotted the arm of his chair back into place.

Watsonville very slowly stood up, walked the distance between the desks, then, just as slowly, gave Hippo the book. As he returned to his seat, he almost staggered. His appearance was the epitome of terror. By now everyone was mightily intrigued. What on earth could exist between those black covers that it was a death sentence if Hippo found out? Photos of naked men and women copulating? An extremely lewd pornographic story? Knowing Watsonville's character, either of these explanations was quite probable.

Hippo flicked over the pages, a puzzled expression on his face. Then he frowned. 'What's it all mean?' he asked. He put his spectacles on, turned over a few more pages, then read some of it aloud. 'Calum Swabey. Eight and a half. Then we have a letter, a capital C. Thick. Good. One shilling and sixpence. John Durrant. Four. Then a capital U. Droops. Not good. Three shillings.' Absolute silence. Never had a class of Hippo's been so quiet. 'Paul Aylott. Six. C. Average. Quick and nervous. Two shillings and sixpence. Oh, here's Calum Swabey again. Nine. Gone up, apparently. C. Thick. Vigorous, experienced, animal. Gratis.' I felt very alarmed. Agate had been absent from school the previous week with flu. Tuesday morning I felt randy, and suddenly lust was stronger than aesthetics. I gave Muckley half a crown, and at lunchtime descended

35

the stairs to the cloakroom. I did the same thing on Wednesday, Thursday and Friday, as Watson's technical skills proved to be wonderfully expert. But I didn't tell Stephen; had no intentions of doing so: let sleeping cocks lie. Now, if Hippo read out whatever it said on the subject of Alan Nancekievill, there would be, to put it mildly, trouble.

'Roy Johns,' Hippo continued. 'Six and a half. U. Big head. Takes ages. Two shillings and sixpence. Are you big-headed, Johns? I was under the impression you had a rather low opinion of yourself. But you certainly take ages when it comes to handing in your homework. What is this about? Some kind of betting list? Are you all gambling on the horses?'

'It's private,' Watsonville stuttered. 'Can I have it back, please sir?'

The bell for the end of the lesson rang at this point, which broke the tension; we began to put books away, hurriedly. Those boys whose names had been read out were furious, and many others, who guessed there were statistics in the book concerning themselves, seemed none too happy, either. Watson would be fortunate to get to the next lesson in one piece, and, as for after school, he would be lucky if he didn't get killed. Calum Swabey, who looked like murder personified, was a huge hairy gorilla, over six feet tall, the first fifteen's prop forward. He could smash anybody into the middle of next week unassisted; with the rest of the class helping, Watsonville would be pulp before he could land in the middle of next week.

'No,' said Hippo. 'You can't have it back. Not till I've found out what it all means. I'm confiscating it.' He levered himself up from his chair, lumbered over to his desk, put the book in a drawer, locked it, and slipped the key into his attaché case. 'Now get out of here, the lot of you. You're a bunch of morons.'

'Incredible!' Stephen said to me, as we walked down the corridor. 'Never heard anything like it!' His eyes were shining. 'Thank God you and I won't be mentioned!'

'Yes. Thank God.'

'What's C and U stand for, do you think? Circumcised and uncircumcised?'

'I guess so.'

'Sounds as if Calum has an impressive quantity of apparatus.'

'Performing more than adequately, too,' I said. 'Though it's only Watsonville's opinion. How does he know the sizes? He can't very well sit in the dark down there, measuring.'

'Guesswork.'

'Wonder who else has it free. You know . . . I'd love to read that book!'

'So would I,' Stephen said. Then, after a pause, he murmured, 'Calum Swabey . . . nine!'

'I hope you aren't going to do some detective work on whether it's a fact.'

'Of course not! I love you.'

'Ssssh!' We were just by Richard Pepperell's classroom; his door was open, and he was sitting at his desk, waiting to teach us English, the final lesson of the day.

'You're late!' he barked. 'Where the devil are the rest of you?'

Watsonville's body wasn't completely pulped by the battering to which it was subjected after school, though he went home with a swollen eye and a generally roughed-up appearance. (Muckley vanished from Pepperell's class so quickly when the bell rang that he got off unscathed.) But Eric's career as a whore was ruined. No one, ever again, went down into the cloakroom for a lunchtime servicing. Decency and propriety had been violated. Outraged! Of course it was more or less known who was a customer of Watsonville's and who was not, and whether they were frequent or infrequent patrons, but those comments on size and performance, written in a book that was read aloud to the class by Hippo of all people, were a gross intrusion into an area of existence that should have been absolutely private. Sacred. Hippo, remembering that the only moment in his lessons when you could have heard a pin drop was when he perused Watsonville's accounts, now developed the unpleasant habit, when the din became too much, of unlocking his drawer and reading a few entries. 'John Barraclough. Beyond belief. U. Black as soot. Twice. Gratis.' The technique worked: silence was instantaneous. So was the renewal of Watsonville's terror; and a beating-up after school also inevitably followed. I quaked whenever Hippo opened the book: surely this time he would spell out the details of Alan Nancekievill's equipment and its functional capacities, and Stephen would know. On these occasions I said to myself: some-how that object must be removed from Hippo's clutches. Other boys thought so too. Calum Swabey certainly did, for after one of these embarrassing, nail-biting sessions, he said to me as we walked down the corridor, 'How the fuck can we get hold of it?'

'I've no idea,' I said.

'Burglary,' Stephen suggested.

'That requires nicking Hippo's key. Which is well nigh impossible.'

'One of these days I'm going to make mincemeat of that fucker, Watsonville!' Calum said. 'I'll tear his scrotum right off and stuff it down his gullet!' With that crude and chilling threat, he stomped into Pepperell's classroom and tried to compose himself for a lesson on imagery in *A Midsummer Night's Dream*.

I couldn't concentrate on Oberon and Titania either; my mind kept straying back to the key in Hippo's attaché case. Eventually, the glimmerings of a plan came to me, then its chief outlines, and as the bell went for the end of school, its details. It could work. Yes: and it *should* work. But I needed somebody else to help. Not Stephen. He mustn't be allowed near the black book; he'd want to read it. Why not Calum Swabey? Hairy gorilla he might be, but he also had brains.

I told Stephen I couldn't walk home with him that evening; I had errands to do for my mother, which lay in the opposite direction.

'What errands?' he asked. 'You never said.'

'Shopping,' I replied, vaguely. 'She's not feeling too good . . . and somebody has to buy the groceries.'

'Oh.' He looked disappointed. 'Well . . . I'll see you tomorrow.'

I waited till he had left the premises, then went in search of Calum, who was in the changing-rooms pulling on his rugby shorts. He listened to my idea, and said, 'It's worth a try. Let's see if Hippo is still in his room.'

'I thought you were about to kick balls around.'

'It's not an official practice. Just a few of us belting leather. Come on . . . no time like the present!'

Hippo *was* still in his room, at his desk, marking exercise books. He was humming tunelessly, and fiddling with his buttons, not bothering now, as there was no one else there, to cover himself with Harrap's Standard French Dictionary. The chair arm was lying on the floor. We could see all this, because we had crept up to his door and found it ajar.

'O.K.,' I breathed. 'Fingers crossed. Let's give it a whirl.' Calum nodded. He strolled up the corridor, then stopped. When Hippo came out, he would be walking back, looking as if he was on his way to the rugby practice; and when Hippo had passed him, turned the corner and disappeared out of sight, he would stand by the classroom door: my watch-dog, to warn me of Hippo's return.

I knocked, and went in. 'Mr Clapton, sir! You're wanted on the telephone!'

Hippo stared at me balefully, eyes peeping over the top of his spectacles. 'Telephone?' he queried. 'Where? Which one?'

'In the secretaries' office.' (It was a conveniently long distance away.) 'Urgent, Mrs Booker said.'

'Humph. Thank you, Nancekievill.' He heaved himself up and waddled out of the room, quite unsuspecting. I pretended to go in the opposite direction; then, as he turned the corner, I dashed back. Calum was already waiting at the door. 'What the hell are you going to think of,' he hissed, 'when he says tomorrow there wasn't a phone call?'

'I'll think of something,' I answered, as I hurried into the classroom.

The attaché case was on the desk. And open. Great! Soon we would have it. The plan was to remove the key, unlock the drawer and steal the book before Hippo returned. But I couldn't find the key. The attaché case was full of books and papers, and I didn't want to disturb them too much: Hippo might guess his property had been tampered with. I fumbled around. It wasn't there. It had to be!

'Hurry up!' Calum said.

'I can't find the fucking thing!'

No help for it; I would have to empty the case. Text books, exercise books, a copy of Zola's *Germinal*: a half-eaten apple, yesterday's *Daily Telegraph*, three cigarette ends (whatever were they doing in there?), old bus tickets, a packet of potato crisps, letters, bills, and – the dirty old man! – a magazine on the cover of which was a naked woman with positively gargantuan knockers.

'He's coming!' Calum whispered, and sped off down the corridor.

Eureka! There it was, at the bottom! I grabbed it, pushed everything else back into the case, then picked up some papers from the rubbish bin seconds before Hippo trundled in. 'What are you doing, Nancekievill?' he asked.

'I left some work here this afternoon,' I said, and pointed to the papers I was holding.

'What was all this about a phone call? There was nobody in the office when I got there, and the phone was *on* the hook.'

'Did I say the secretaries' office?' I tried to make my expression look like the ultimate in regret and concern; I even banged my forehead with the hand clutching the papers. 'I am so sorry! I meant the masters' common room. I . . . do hope it wasn't important.'

Hippo glared at me, the piggy eyes full of suspicion. 'It was probably news of my brother; he's in hospital. I don't even know the number to call back! You're a blithering idiot, Nancekievill. A moron. A cretin. What are you?'

'A blithering idiot, sir, *and* a moron *and* a cretin.'

'It's time you pulled your socks up.' Cheekily, I did so. 'Get out, boy!' he yelled. 'Get out!'

He could easily have discovered the hospital's number in the telephone directory, I thought as I fled, or dialled inquiries; *he's* the one who's a cretin. Calum was waiting for me outside the building, on the lawn. 'Here it is,' I said, and showed him the key. 'But I didn't have time to open the drawer.'

'Mar-vell-ous!' He leaped up and down, hugged me, lifted me clean into the air, then for some reason we were rolling over and over on the lawn, which had been mown that afternoon; I ended up underneath him, my clothes and hair sprinkled with grass cuttings, wilting daisies and withered buttercups, and smelling sweetly of dried flowers. He lay on me for a few moments, almost pressing me to death he was so heavy. Then he got up and said, 'I seem to have an erection.'

I grinned. 'So have I.'

He brushed the dead grass off his white shorts. 'We can't do anything about it here! Well . . . we have the key, but we don't have the book. What next, Superbrain?'

'We somehow have to get back into Hippo's room.'

'What are you doing this evening? We could try when it's dark.'

'Why not tomorrow during the day? Damn sight easier than breaking into the school after dark!'

'Hippo's room is on the ground floor. Haven't you ever noticed that his window doesn't shut properly? The catch is missing. We could climb in that way.'

'It's a very small window,' I said.

'Yes. Still . . . *you* could squeeze through; you're much slimmer than I am. I'll give you a bunk-up, then stay outside to keep watch. And . . . when you've got the book . . . we could do something pleasant with these erections.'

Nine, C, thick, vigorous, experienced, animal. 'O.K.,' I said. 'What time?'

'It's dark about eight. Eight thirty any good?'

'Sure.'

I did some thinking at tea-time; so much that my mother remarked on it: I must be in love, she said. My thoughts were not on that subject, however. The prospective burglary, and nine, C, thick, etcetera were my preoccupations, and what were we going to do with the black book when we had removed it from Hippo's drawer? Calum would almost certainly demand that it should be destroyed – perhaps say burn it, or throw it in the river, or drop it into the nearest dustbin. I didn't want that at all. I wanted to read the whole thing from cover to cover. It shouldn't be too difficult to organize, I decided.

I set off at eight o'clock, armed with a torch. It was a cloudy, moonless night, and, not daring to use the torch in the school grounds in case anyone saw the glow, I found myself stumbling almost blindly in the pitch blackness. Calum was waiting for me by Hippo's window: he heard my footsteps and whispered, 'I'm here!'

'Where?'

He touched me: I was standing right beside him. I then touched him; let my hands wander down his body. 'Later,' he said. 'We've got work to do first.'

'Are Watsonville's assessments accurate?' I asked.

'You'll have to form your own opinion.'

'Do you *want* my opinion?'

He did not answer, so I took this as an invitation to go ahead: unbuttoned him, began to finger it. Limp, but it was soon coaxed to life. Calum unzipped my jeans. 'We shouldn't be doing this,' he said, as he started to fondle my cock.

'Why ever not?'

'We should be screwing women. That's what it's for.'

'It's for whatever you want to do with it.'

'And how will Agate react?' he asked.

'He isn't going to find out.'

'Good. Tell me . . . do you really prefer boys? You're actually in love with Agate?'

'Yes,' I said. 'To both questions.'

'I don't understand you! I want to do this with a girl. I know quite a few, as it happens . . . I've been going out with girls since I was fourteen . . . but I can't imagine how you get round to . . . to asking them if. . .'

42

'Beyond Belief Barraclough says exactly the same.'

'Oh? You've done it with him, too?'

We were silent after that; just devoted ourselves to bringing each other to a sensational conclusion. 'God! I enjoyed that!' I said, as I allowed it to fertilise the shrubs under Hippo's window. 'You great big animal!' I was panting, weak at the knees.

Calum, too, was gasping. 'You're pretty good, I must say,' he said. 'I wonder if Watsonville would agree . . . but you aren't in his book, I guess.'

'I am. That's why I want to get hold of it.'

'Are you!' Calum was surprised. 'And Agate isn't aware of that?'

'No. He isn't.'

We rescued our jeans from around our ankles, and began to set in motion the evening's other important business. He lifted me up; I jerked at the window, which, as he had said, was not shut properly, and a minute later I was inside the classroom.

That was the only time I did it with Calum. Occasionally in bed with Stephen – in every long-term relationship, so I'm told, one or other partner now and then will fantasise – I would think about Calum the animal. He found a wife when he was twenty-two, produced four children, and went into politics. Conservative M.P. for somewhere or other in Hertfordshire, and he even had a brief spell as junior minister at Overseas Development. You see him from time to time on TV, on programmes like *Panorama* or *World in Action*: dark wavy hair, neat blue suit, blue shirt, blue tie. Another identikit Tory; the soul, you would think, of middle-class, middle-aged, conventional British respectability.

With the torch to give me light, I had the drawer open in seconds, found the book, and slipped it into the inside pocket of my jacket. Calum couldn't see this; the bottom of the window was seven feet from the ground, and I blessed the Victorian builders who, so Hippo had informed us in one of his many digressions, constructed school windows like this so the pupils couldn't be disturbed by whatever was going on outside. I pretended to continue the search: opened and shut the drawer, rustled papers, moved books.

'What's the matter?' Calum asked, in a loud whisper. 'What's gone wrong?'

'I can't find it.'

'What!'

'I can't find it!'

'It must be there. It has to be there!'

'It isn't.'

'Well . . . look on the bookshelves. In the cupboards. The top of the cupboards.'

I obeyed. 'It is not in this room,' I said in a very definite sort of voice, ten minutes later. 'It's gone.'

'How? Why? It can't have gone!'

'Perhaps Hippo's taken it home. Or even chucked it away. Or . . . do you think somebody else might have stolen it? It's not just you and me interested in its contents.'

'How can anyone else have stolen it, you fool! *We've* got the key!'

'True. Well . . . he must have taken it home.'

'Shit! Bugger! *Fuck*!! What do we do now?'

'Nothing we can do.' I climbed onto the window-sill. 'Listen . . . there's no point in me staying in here. I'm coming out.' I pushed myself through the narrow space of the window, and stood on Calum's hands. He took my whole weight effortlessly, and lowered me to the ground.

'What a stupid farce!' he said, gloomily.

'Not altogether. We still have the key, so . . . we can try again, some other time. If Hippo has taken it home, he'll put it back when he's finished with it. He keeps all the stuff he confiscates in that drawer. Look. I've brought you a present.'

'I can't see in the dark.'

'Your cigarette lighter.' Calum had been flicking it on and off in a lesson two months ago, and Hippo had removed it.

'Thanks.' He said nothing more as we crept out of the school grounds; he seemed slumped in depression. Then, just before our ways parted, he said, trying to cheer himself up I imagine, 'I suppose I can still have the pleasure of ripping Watsonville's balls off. Well . . . goodnight.'

'See you tomorrow,' I said. I raced home, told my parents I was going to bed early to revise for a French test, then made some cocoa and took it, with a packet of biscuits and the stolen book, up to my room. I searched for the pages on which my name appeared, curious to know Watsonville's opinion. Here it was: 'Alan Nancekievill. Six and a half. U. Thick. Daredevil.' The descriptions of my other performances were 'amusing,' 'uninhibited,' and 'he loves it.'

I began to read from the beginning. It was an absorbing document, containing all sorts of information about people I'd known for years; but which, however close in some cases the friendship between us was, I would never have found out in a lifetime. I was amazed, too, to think of the money Watsonville had earned. Some of it went to Muckley for his pimping; that was the explanation of all those pricy tickets for Covent Garden. (He had not been in the past few weeks, despite productions of *Tristan and Isolde* and *Gotterdämmerung*; couldn't afford it now, presumably.) I don't know how Watson spent the money. Maybe put it in a bank.

I was thoroughly enjoying myself until I turned a page and saw one of the entries for February the twenty-third: 'Stephen Agate. Six. C. Average. Writhes, flops, moans. Two shillings and sixpence.' WHAT!!! Was that the week *I* had flu? I racked my brains: it was, I was sure of it. The week before half-term I had been ill, confined in bed from the Sunday evening to the Thursday afternoon. Another page, then another: yes, Stephen had also been a patron on February the twenty-fourth, twenty-fifth, twenty-sixth *and* twenty-seventh, one more time than I had been when *he* had flu; for each visit paying the standard rate (serve him right, little two-timing bastard – after my first session I had got it cut-price), and the comments about him were more beta than the alpha pluses Calum, Beyond Belief Barraclough and I had obtained: 'Charming,' 'delicate,' 'nice,' 'O.K.'

Love is without logic. It puts the adored one on far too high a pedestal. *I* might have strayed from the monogamous path that Cupid (particularly at seventeen) requires, not only with Watsonville but Calum Swabey and John Barraclough as well, but for Stephen to do it: that was intolerable. You know how weak you are – selfish, mean, lustful – but the beloved is perfect; that is why, at seventeen at any rate, you love him: he is the embodiment of all beauty, goodness and truth. That is what Agate meant to me. The more ordinary, more durable qualities like strength of character, compatibility, shared interests, similar sense of humour, etcetera, etcetera, can make relationships last, and with us they did; but the night I read Watsonville's black book, Stephen, as the embodiment of all beauty, goodness and truth, no longer existed. I was furious, madly jealous, and, more than anything else, terribly hurt that my ideals had proved to be illusions. I cried myself to sleep that night.

I never told him. What would have been the point? If I had done so, I would have been forced to confess that I too had erred, and the mutual recriminations would perhaps have damaged things irrevocably. It was a question of saving what was worthwhile, and when I considered, during the next few weeks, what *was* worthwhile, I found there was no way I wanted to abandon Stephen. My little agate stone, lustrous, translucent jewel: precious beyond price. (I didn't know then that 'agate' also means 'astray.') Where would I find another? I didn't want another. I wanted *him*, warts and all. So I swallowed the hard pellet of my anger, jealousy and hurt, lived with its bitter taste for a while, and gradually it dissolved.

'What is the matter?' he asked, more than once.

'Nothing,' I lied. 'I'm a bit depressed. It's not important.'

He accepted that. Depression, I found, is a helpful term to use about oneself from time to time. It stops people probing; they have little desire to shoulder the burdens of others. They usually say 'Oh' and change the subject.

What to do about Watsonville's book? And Hippo's key. The latter was easily dealt with. I gave it to Hippo at the end of a lesson one afternoon, and said, 'I found this on the floor just now.' He obviously recognized what key it was, for he looked puzzled, glanced at his desk, then at his attaché case; but he suspected nothing, merely said, 'Thank you.' If he should think, when he discovered the book was missing, that I was connected with its disappearance, I would simply lie my way out of the situation. He couldn't prove I was responsible. Before I gave him the key, however, I did wonder whether to return the book to the drawer, but that was a moment of sheer stupidity. I had saved the class agonies of embarrassment, including myself and, I suppose, Stephen: I didn't want anyone to go on being tortured. Stephen must have sweated as much as I did each time it was read aloud, but such a good actor was he that I never noticed his fear. The toad! The cheat! What a Judas Iscariot! Would I ever trust him again? How many lies had he told me since we first made love? How many other boys had he been with? Doubts such as these bothered me for ages. Until the day came when I said to myself: none of this matters. I love Stephen. It's the only thing of importance.

I could have destroyed the book. I could have given it back to Watsonville; it was his property. But I didn't think he deserved it. It gave me no pleasure to keep it, though that is what I did. I threw it into the bottom of a cupboard. I salvaged it when I finally left home at the age of twenty-one, and I've been aware of it in subsequent moves; but it was only on Tuesday, when I was sorting out the attic, that I re-read it. It seemed pointless not to say anything to Stephen – after all these years it was supremely insignificant that Nancekievill was recorded therein four times and Agate five.

Hippo soon found that he had been burgled. Noise levels shot up again one morning, and he unlocked the drawer. Peered, then grunted. He pulled the drawer right out, put it on the desk and searched through it. The class became silent, and dared to hope. 'Where the hell has it gone?' he muttered, and the class was jubilant. He searched a bit longer, then shrugged his shoulders, replaced the drawer and locked it. He resumed his disquisition on Ho Chi Minh, whom he claimed to have met in Hanoi at the end of the War, and looked at me several times, rather quizzically. The bogus telephone call, the finding of the key. He wasn't completely devoid of intelligence. But he said nothing: he had no proof.

He continued to say nothing, but from then on I discovered I had to behave with absolute propriety in Hippo's lessons. If I talked out of turn, I was pounced on. If my work was less than average, I was the object of scorn and derision, and made to do it again. Well, I could accept all that: it was the price I had to pay for saving the class from public recitals of everyone's debaucheries. I convinced myself that I was a hero and a martyr.

Now that the book seemed to have vanished off the face of the earth, people gradually became reconciled to Watsonville and Muckley. The desire to tear them limb from limb had, in any case, long since subsided; they were merely in perpetual Coventry now – no one had spoken to them for weeks. But we began once again to think that they were human, of the same species as ourselves, that they deserved similar treatment to ourselves. I led the way; I could afford to of course, having stolen the book and been the agent of rescue, even though neither of these facts was known. I was quite affable to both of them.

I talked about opera with Muckley; he was an expert: had far more knowledge of the subject than I possessed. He asked me what were my favourite operas, and when I said *La Bohème*, *Il Trovatore* and *Billy Budd*, he superciliously replied, 'Oh, you'll soon grow out of *that*!' I retorted that Wagner's music suffered from both dropsy and elephantiasis. He looked really shocked for a moment, then invited me to go with him to Covent Garden to see *The Flying Dutchman* and be proved wrong. I accepted, and was looking forward to the event, but the tickets never materialised. Muckley was still broke. (After marrying his Brunnhilde, he got a job with the Decca record company. The ultimate in bliss, he said: it provided him with masses of Wagner records, free.) Watsonville was a less interesting person. The only subject on which he was an expert was sex, cock being the area in which he was a model research student and postgraduand. But cock, as a conversation piece, has its longueurs. I'd rather spend my time practising on the specimens than in verbally dissecting their merits and defects.

One topic, however, which they both liked to discuss was the disappearance of the black book. 'Hippo was as surprised as we were that it wasn't in his drawer,' said Muckley. 'There's only one answer: theft.' He giggled. 'You know in lavatories on trains there is always a notice that says, "Gentlemen lift the seat"? I wondered the other day – are British Railways ordering men to steal them?'

'Ha-ha,' I said. 'Ha bloody ha.'

Watsonville's reaction to Muckley's little joke was a blank stare; he evidently didn't understand it. 'Who would want to nick such a thing?'

'The book,' Muckley asked, 'or the toilet seat?'

'The book, you arsehole.'

'Someone we all know. And he's probably destroyed it.'

I nodded. 'It's the obvious explanation.'

Watsonville sighed. 'The end of a very lucrative business, alas.'

'And a good thing too,' I said. 'Don't you realise it's against the law to solicit for immoral purposes? People get put in jail for running vice rings.'

'Just because it's against the law,' Muckley said, 'doesn't mean to say it's wrong. There was a demand, so we offered a service. We didn't have a single disappointed customer demanding his money back: most people thought so well of us they came a second time, a third. You came four times yourself, Nancekievill. You don't have any grumbles, do you?'

'No. But I would have if Agate had found out.'

Watsonville and Muckley glanced at each other, throwing all kinds of signals back and forth. I pretended not to notice, but I guessed they were thinking, 'if he knew Stephen had been one of our clients he'd be bashing our heads in.'

'Agate didn't find out,' Watsonville said.

'I don't think prostitution is morally wrong,' I said. 'I agree with you there. If there's a demand, why not supply a service? If the parties are willing, and no hurt is occasioned to either, then nothing's amiss. But don't you think it's all somewhat . . . tasteless? There must have been quite a few people you didn't particularly like doing it with, Eric.'

'No. A cock is always interesting.'

'*Any* cock?'

'Yes.'

'Well, I don't agree with you at all. Some are interesting. Calum's, for instance, or Beyond Belief Barraclough's. But mostly they aren't.'

'Oh-ho!' said Muckley. 'You've had the pleasure of those two, have you?'

'I didn't say that, did I? Eric . . . would you enjoy sex with Hippo?'

They hooted with laughter at this idea. Watsonville shuddered, and said, 'Revolting thought!'

'Point proven, then. Isn't it?'

'People like Hippo don't have sex. They're far too old. Too busy impressing Uncle Ho.'

I remembered the woman with the almighty tits on the magazine cover in Hippo's attaché case. 'Of course he's not too old,' I said. 'And I bet he never even saw Ho Chi Minh. It's much more likely he was in one of Hanoi's brothels.'

'You are a cynic,' Muckley said. Not unadmiringly.

'Just a realist,' I answered.

It was a realistic assumption that Stephen, three decades later, wouldn't be bothered that I had discovered as a result of my theft of the black book – venerable and battered now with age, even mildewed in parts – that he had allowed Watsonville to bring him to orgasm, and realistic, too, to think it wouldn't matter a fuck to him that I had let Watsonville do the same to me. I couldn't have been more wrong. I have never seen him so upset, hurt and angry. It was the biggest crisis of our thirty years: for a few hours it even looked as if our marriage would end in a divorce.

'Our whole relationship has been built on a lie!' he yelled. 'God! When Hippo read those names out I was so scared mine would be among them! I used to say to myself . . . Alan will *kill* me. *He* wouldn't do this evil thing I've done! It never, never, for one moment, occurred to me as I lay in bed with flu that you were *prancing* down to that cloakroom to stick your cock in Watsonville's mouth! Ugh! You're disgusting! Vile! How *could* you? I've looked up to you, worshipped you all these years because I thought you loved me so much! I believed you were *incapable* of doing that!'

'I *did* love you,' I said. 'I *do* love you.'

'Then why did you do it?'

'For the same reason as you. I was randy. At seventeen, eighteen, boys get randy five or six times a day.'

'But I *loathed* myself afterwards! I felt unclean for . . . for weeks! Every time you kissed me, every time we had sex . . . I said to myself, "Poor Alan, *dear* Alan . . . he is so good, and kind, and marvellous, and he doesn't know that this creature he loves is a rotten orange!" "Give not this rotten orange to your friend," Claudio says in *Much Ado About Nothing*. We were doing that play with Pepperell.'

'*A Midsummer Night's Dream*,' I corrected.

'You're the one with the hopeless memory.'

'*A Midsummer Night's Dream*! I remember saying to Calum –'

'The point I'm trying to make is you *didn't* loathe yourself. See here' – he jabbed at the relevant pages, and once again I wished I'd never heard of Watsonville's foul book, never seen it – 'It says "daredevil." I'll give you *daredevil*! Hah! "He loves it." Loves it more than me is the plain truth of it all!'

'Don't be so ridiculous! I'm quite prepared to admit I didn't loathe myself . . . I wanted sex, and somebody else's tongue feels a lot better than my own hand. I wasn't ashamed of it then, and I'm not ashamed of it now. I *enjoyed* it.'

In answer, he hurled a saucepan at me. (We were standing in the kitchen.) I ducked, and it sailed right over my head. Unfortunately, it had cold stew in it from

51

yesterday's dinner which made a large splat on the wall. The mess began to drip slowly down onto the radiator. I had painted that wall, indeed the whole kitchen, only a month previously. He picked up another saucepan, this one containing the remnants of a cauliflower. 'Don't do it!' I warned, but he moved slightly as if to throw it; I sprang at him, seized his arms, and twisted them up behind his back: 'My muscles may not be as vigorous as they were, but they're still *three* times the size of yours! Drop that saucepan.'

'No.'

'Do as I tell you.'

'No!'

I manoeuvred him round so that he was facing away from me, propelled him over to the sink, then pushed his head down till it was a few inches under the tap. Leaning against his arse began to give me an erection. 'Drop that saucepan,' I repeated. He did so. 'I've a good mind to pull your knickers off and screw you right here,' I said.

'It's shut till further notice. Closed for major repairs.'

'Are you being serious?'

'Yes.'

I let him go. 'In that case, I'll be forced to look for it elsewhere.'

'That sums up your whole attitude to me perfectly! I've been used! All along the line. You couldn't get it when I was ill thirty years ago, so you waltzed off to somebody else. You don't really want *me*. You never did! You just want a convenient mouth or hole in which to park your cock and shoot.'

'That is true of every single fuck I've had in my life *except* with you! Why are you . . . distorting everything? It's *obscene!*'

He took a beer from the fridge, opened it, and drank. 'Because I'm hurt, Alan! What do you think these revelations do to *me*? Well? They cause a great deal of pain! For thirty years I had no idea you knew what I did with that . . . that vampire, and it's very hard for me to accept! Why didn't you say so at the time? Weren't you hurt? Wasn't your trust shaken? No. You weren't upset at all, not bothered one little bit. You carried on as if nothing had happened! And why? Only one possible reason. So long as you could have me to poke, you didn't care about anything else! You are such a fucking egoist you have no *idea* what goes on inside me! A self-centred, self-absorbed, cold, hard, humourless, vain, pompous prick of a fucking egoist! Me, me, me, me, *me*! You don't know what love is. You never did, you don't now, and you never will!'

I was baffled. This torrent of abuse couldn't simply be caused by a trivial little incident – a boy relieving us of our sperm – that had taken place before the Suez Crisis, Hungary, Profumo, Harolds Macmillan and Wilson, flower power and hippies, colour TV, at a time when a bus ride was threepence (old money), when gays were illegal, when chocolate had only just come off the ration, when James Dean was starring in *East of Eden* and Jimmy Young was at the top of the hit parade singing the *Unchained Melody*. It was an excuse, a catalyst, a last straw; grievances that had been allowed to stockpile were now exploding all over the place like bombs. What grievances? I didn't know. 'What do you intend to do about it?' I asked.

'I'm leaving.'

'Don't be such a silly ass. Where do you imagine you'll go?'

'To my sister's.'

'Isabel? Oh yes, all girls together! And I expect Mummy will be there too? Knitting needles and tea-cups akimbo! Well, I shall do something a bit more *male*!! Il faut cultiver notre whatever it was, as Voltaire said. I'm going to spend the afternoon digging that garden so thoroughly that when you come back you'll be lucky to find *anything* left of your precious rose trees!'

'I'm not coming back.'

I laughed. 'I expect you'll stop over for dinner; Isabel's a pretty good cook. But you'll be c-*rawling* in here at bedtime!'

Stephen slammed the beer can on the counter and walked out.

It was a pleasant afternoon in the garden – mild April weather: daffodils, tulips, the sweet smell of the year's first cut grass. My flabby muscles ached in a satisfactory sort of way, and felt just a little less flabby. I went indoors at six o'clock, washed the stew off the kitchen wall, then had a bath. I cooked my dinner and drank a bottle of wine. Before going to bed I watched an old film on the telly, another memento of the fifties: *All About Eve*, Bette Davis at the height of her career. My last thoughts, as I was dropping off to sleep, were that I'd get woken up in an hour or two by Stephen slipping in beside me, and had I left the hall light on for him?

Half past eight; a cheerful, sunny Sunday morning. No Stephen. I got out of bed, dressed, and looked in the other rooms. The hall light was still on: he hadn't come back. I panicked a bit at this point, thinking something disastrous could have occurred, and I phoned Isabel.

'He didn't even stay to dinner,' she said. 'He left at about . . . oh . . . five thirty. I assumed he was going home. What's up? Have you two been quarrelling?'

'Didn't he tell you?'

'Tell me what?'

'That we had . . . er . . . been quarrelling.'

'No. What was it about?'

'Nothing serious,' I said. 'Was Mother-in-law with you when Stephen was there?'

'Who? Oh, *my* mother. Yes.'

'Where the hell is he, then?'

'Alan, you don't think anything dreadful –'

'Of course not.' Pause. 'Isabel . . . do *you* think. . . ?'

'No!'

'I was wondering if I should phone the police. But it would sound odd . . . a man of forty-seven doesn't come home and another *man* worries about it. They'll probably ask what business it is of mine. I can't very well say he's my lover! It's this department of life where we gays always lose out, etcetera, etcetera, etcetera.'

'I'll phone for you.'

She did. The police had no dossier on a Stephen Agate, and there had been no accidents or violent deaths in our area last night in which identification of corpses had been impossible. They asked for a description of Stephen's

54

appearance and the clothes he had been wearing, and said they would call if there was any news.

This Sunday was not the most tranquil day of my existence: he had never stopped out all night without my knowing where and why. Or even, on the infrequent occasions it had happened in the long-ago past, with whom. I attempted to busy myself with work in the garden, but time dragged. Isabel and I phoned each other, repeatedly. At lunchtime I went to the pub, but I was back in the house after only one beer; he might have come in, or the phone might ring. Late in the afternoon, the key turned in the lock.

'Where the fuck have you been?' I demanded.

'Leigh-on-sea.'

'*Leigh-on-sea!* What on earth for?'

'Oh . . . I stayed with an old friend. Noel; you remember him, don't you? We . . . walked down to the cockle boats, had a few drinks, and stared at the sea. Rough and glittering it was. What skies they have down there! Vast! These black, rushing clouds, and a chimney just visible on the Kent coast – the oil refinery at Sheerness, I imagine. It all looked a bit like that Turner painting; what is it? The one in the National. *Rain, Steam and Speed*? Well . . . it blew a few cobwebs away.' He sounded too jaunty, which meant that underneath he was forlorn: tail-between-the-legs.

'Why didn't you phone? I've been worried sick!'

'I wanted to . . . hurt you.'

'But what have I *done*?'

'Nothing,' he said. 'Nothing.'

'I'm in the dark, Stephen!'

'I know it's all very childish. Getting hot under the collar about something that happened all those years ago. . . It wasn't that, really. Watsonville's book was a trigger.'

'So I assumed.'

'The past few months . . . we've been taking each other too much for granted. I've been fed up, Alan! You've made me feel flat. Pedestrian. And me you, I suppose. I got to thinking about the things I might have done if you'd never wanted me. The men I could have been with . . . all those doors I never opened into

55

the rose garden. Call it a thirty-year itch. Well, I've scratched it. It's gone.'

'Did you have sex with anyone last night? I wouldn't want us to get AIDS.'

'Of course not! I cuddled up with Noel, but we didn't do anything.' He put his arms round me and kissed me. 'I'm sorry. I really am . . . sorry. Causing you all that –'

'It's not important. We'll forget it.'

'That's one of your greatest qualities: you've always been able to forgive. It is, isn't it, one of the hardest things to do in life? I admire you for it. I love you for it.'

Then we both said, together, 'Least said, soonest mended,' and laughed. It was my line really, but in thirty years of sharing, the next bit of dialogue can often be predictable. I'd said it before, more than once. And would doubtless say it again.

'I love you,' I said. 'It's all that matters.' I'd said that, too. 'But you ought to make your peace with Isabel.'

'Isabel?'

'I phoned her. Thinking you might be there. She's . . . a little concerned. While you're doing that, I could cook the dinner. Roast lamb followed by gooseberry pie. O.K.? And a bottle of Chateauneuf du Pape. Afterwards . . . I'll take you to bed, and try to be very tender and loving. Lots of caresses and kisses. Not the usual Nancekievill bull-in-a-china-shop-bang-bang-animal-fuck-fuck-fuck.'

'But I like the usual Nancekievill bull-in-a-china-shop-bang-bang-animal-fuck-fuck-fuck.' He started to sing: *Nobody does it better*.

I smiled. 'I guess I can manage that then, *and* try a little tenderness.'

'Sounds like a good evening.'

'First of all I want to show you something.' I led him into the kitchen, and he glanced at the clean wall. Then I pointed out of the window.

'A pile of garden rubbish?'

'The result of my labours yesterday. Leaves, sticks, dead flowers, privet cuttings, the branch that fell off the plum tree in November, and . . . right on the top is a book. Watsonville's famous black book.'

His eyes lit up. 'You think a cremation appropriate? Why not!'

'I'll soak it all in paraffin, and you can strike the ritual match. Suttee, however, is forbidden.'

He laughed. 'You surely can't imagine anyone would throw themselves on a funeral pyre for Watsonville!'

So the book was destroyed at last, and the malevolent ghosts its contents had conjured up were laid to rest. It took some while to burn; nineteen fifties paper was tougher than nineteen eighties fallen leaves. 'I wonder what happened to Hippo,' I said, as I watched the pages blacken.

'Buried long since, I guess,' Stephen replied. 'Down in Hell, talking to Stalin.'

'He'd be seventy-odd if he's still alive. Could be in a bungalow in Peacehaven. Sunset Homes for Elderly Distressed Gentlefolk. When you're old and incontinent, I shall put you in a similar institution – a hotel for Distressed Gentlegays.'

'Beyond Belief Barraclough. Why did we call him that?'

'Because. . .' To remind him, I thought, could hold up the exorcism, so I said, 'I don't remember. He was a Nigerian. A Biafran, to be precise, even though he had an English name. He was a colonel in Ojukwu's army during the Civil War, and got killed.'

'Look!' He pointed at the flames, which were beginning to burn more fiercely; they had thrown a piece of paper, almost uncharred, to one side. We could see quite clearly in Watsonville's inimitable scrawl: 'Calum Swabey. Nine. C. Thick. Vigorous, experienced, animal. Gratis.'

'I think that deserves to broil too.' I picked up a stick, and pushed the offending page back into the hottest part of the fire.

'I wonder if it really was,' Stephen said.

'What?'

'Calum's column. I suppose you never found out?'

This ghost was proving particularly contumacious, I thought; but I was determined it should not live on to start new problems, just as the old ones were being got rid of. 'No,' I lied.

'There was something *bad* about the whole Watsonville business. I'm not quite sure . . . was it, perhaps, a necessary evil?'

The flames were dying down; a thick pall of smoke was now rising from the garden refuse, and the book lay in ashes. 'It wasn't wholly wrong,' I said. 'Morally speaking. It was indiscreet and unsavoury. Not nice. But it's taught you and me a lesson. Can we go inside now? I must parboil the potatoes before I put them in the oven. While I do that, you can phone your sister, then fix me a vodka and orange. Without booze, I'm unable to cook properly.'

Watsonville: requiescat in pace.

COUSINS

1939

In the beginning was before the War. A white dog with black spots, sniffing. The beach. The sun. A banana, its skin strange, like the dog's tail. The sea, high as us after a few steps, green and engulfing; then Aunt Mary's hands pulling Tom out. He screams. He is a baby, my cousin, though he's older than me. I shall catch him up; it's only six months.

I am the Sun King; Tom is the Rainbow. All morning my mother has been cutting out a costume of gold paper and my aunt is now busy with purple and orange. It is for a competition. I'm afraid the pins will prick me, but I won't say so. Now they tell us we must dance barefoot. Tom refuses. But the grown-ups insist, and we dance in front of the judges. *I* dance: Tom just howls and howls. We don't win the prize.

At Aunt Mary's. I am looking out of the window very early in the morning; so is Tom. There are fleecy pink clouds in the sky like fish-scales; down the street trees and houses and telegraph poles are black as I look towards the sun. There is the clop of the milkman's horse. Uncle Philip bursts in, angry, threatening, waving a hair-brush. Was Tom crying, 'grizzling' as my uncle calls it? Or did I drop things with a clatter getting out of bed? I can't remember, but the picture is there, filed away, in my mind.

Mum. I love her more than anyone in the whole

world. I want to help her all I can for she is so busy and so weary. Or so she's always saying. I watch her light the dining-room fire and I push open the coal-box lid for her. Last month I cracked my head open on its edges; they took me to the hospital for stitches. 'What are they doing to my baby cousin?' Tom wailed, tears dirtying his face. Now the fire is alight. 'I need six pairs of hands, Chris,' Mum says, dashing off to the kitchen. Chris, and then Hughes. I wonder why it's that. It's peculiar.

Out in the garden. Soon it will be my birthday. The cherry tree is a white blaze. Tulip petals, streaks like blood, fleck the white grass under the tree. It's hot. There are scalding scents in the air, and sleepy bees. Uncle Philip is not coming on our next holiday. I'm glad; I'm afraid of Uncle Philip, though I don't tell Tom that. The grown-ups are arguing. Aunt Mary is here with suitcases. Mum looks worried and Aunt Mary is crying into her handkerchief. The garden is enormous. There is a pond with water lilies, and a rockery that stretches up and up. In the irises at the back Dad finds a toad. Irises smell of velvet. The toad is sitting on the biggest stone, puffing. It's slimy and its eyes are ugly. I go up by the steps past the lilies and poppies and marigolds. I can't see where the garden ends. There are roses, all colours, and a pear tree and lilac. I'm happy.

Indoors, Tom tries to help my mother. She's asleep on the lounge settee. He clambers onto the kitchen stool. Now he is high enough to reach into the sink. He starts to wash up for her. He doesn't drop a single plate, not even the heavy dish we use for meat. But there isn't time to get down when he wants to wee, and it soaks his trousers. It trickles down his legs, warm and unpleasant. Aunt Mary comes in and smacks him, very hard. He lies on the dining-room floor and screams. He bangs his head on purpose; froth bubbles between his lips. He even stuffs the corner of the carpet into his mouth and tries to choke. Aunt Mary says Hitler does that, and she goes into the garden, humming to herself. Tom won't help again, ever ever ever.

60

Dad is in a deckchair reading the paper. I hit it so he jumps in surprise. We chase up the garden and fall in a heap of laughter. He lifts me so I can see right into the cherry blossom. I'm going to be just like him.

Another holiday. This time we are in a cottage, though it's the same beach. It's much better without Uncle Philip. There are crumbling gold cliffs. I had forgotten they were there. Grandma and Grandpa are with us; Grandpa is deaf and wheezes. He has asthma, and a funny smell, not nice, and I don't like it when he picks me up close to him. Grandma has a very loud voice through shouting too much at Grandpa. She walks with her feet sticking out at ten to two. In a sweet-shop she thumps her umbrella on the counter and yells, 'I want service!' Uncle Philip has come to see Aunt Mary. The other grown-ups talk about him in whispers. He stays a long time, and makes a fuss of Tom. Aunt Mary carries me into the sea. I'm afraid. She is slippery and rubbery like a fish and the water is dark green and I am going to drown. I shriek with terror.

There are strange feelings these days. Dad is angry if I interrupt him when he's listening to the news on the wireless. He's always listening to the news now. It's warm, dry September weather. My mother accidentally drops an egg on the kitchen floor. Dad summons her to the wireless. They listen intently. 'War's broken out,' he says. What is this thing that can break out? I see the jagged halves of the egg-shell, the gluey substance spreading on the floor. Then the sirens wail.

1951

The year of the Festival. Attlee's government falls. Grandma and Grandpa die within a week of each other. She had cancer of the stomach; I was eating an apple when she told Mum the symptoms. I had to throw the apple away. One evening soon after her death I am at Aunt Mary's house, celebrating Tom's birthday. He is very tall now, nearly six feet, with a mop of black hair that hangs over one eye. Bony and pale. An odd, quiet boy who walks by himself. Useless at games. Uncle Philip has sent a card and a present; he always does, though we haven't seen him since the week before the War. He has lived in Nicaragua for many years. There it is on the map, a little blob in the clutter of Central America, oceans away: meaningless. Aunt Mary is trilling on the piano when Dad arrives. He looks very upset about something. 'Mary, can I talk to you?' But my aunt continues to thump out the tune – *Carmencita, Carmencita, queen of all!* – and tells him to wait till she has finished.

What Dad has to say is that he has just come from his parents' house; Grandpa is stretched out on the floor in front of the fire, dead.

I go with friends from school to the Festival. The skylon; the new concert hall: London is being rebuilt. I smoke my first cigarette; it tastes of straw. I phone Mum to tell her I'll be late home – my friends and I are going to walk round the West End and see the bright lights, have a meal somewhere perhaps. Dad answers the phone and says Mum is in bed. I've forgotten that she went to the dentist today to have all her teeth out; the pain, Dad says, is much worse than she imagined beforehand. I feel guilty that I've forgotten; that I'm enjoying myself. This stupid kid from school is in the phone-box with me, putting on a high voice and pretending he's my girlfriend. Fortunately Dad can't hear this.

I don't have a girlfriend, but I'd like one, very much. I think of girls at night as I fall asleep.

This is the last year the holidays are spent at the cottage by the sea: the last year of childhood. Almost every summer I can remember, and that includes all the summers of the War, we have stayed here. The cottage is being sold and the new owners don't want to let it to holiday-makers. It is time to leave it, I think; the rock pools, the surfing waves, the cliff climbs, we have done them so often. Time for something new, something adult. Coming here holds me back in a part of life I want to discard.

I have the first experience of adulthood this summer. Tom and I, as always, share the little room with the twin beds high up under the thatch-eaves. The weather is stiflingly hot: a storm has been brewing for days but still it does not come. Sleep is difficult, virtually impossible. The moon shines in through the window: I can see Tom playing with himself. I'm stiff, just watching. I know about these things from books I have read and through listening and talking to kids at school, though I've never tried to do it, let alone watched anyone else. But if Tom does, why shouldn't I?

It feels . . . fantastic. I think about girls. A girl, any girl . . . Yes!

Tom has seen me. When he has finished too, he says, 'Have you ever done it with anyone else, Chris?'

'Done it . . . with. . . ?'

'I have.'

'You mean . . . you've got a girlfriend?'

'No. Other boys. Well . . . three boys all told.'

I don't answer. I can't; such behaviour is beyond my wildest imaginings.

'You're shocked,' Tom says.

'No.' Which is a lie, of course.

'I'm in love with a boy.'

'How can you love a *boy*?'

'I do.' He sighs, profoundly. 'I sometimes wonder if I'm unique. A quirk of nature.'

After a long silence, I say, 'You must be. Who is this boy?'

'He's at school.'

'Do I know him?'

'No.'

'What does he think about it?'

'I haven't told him. I wouldn't dare.'

Neither of us says anything else. Some time later I realise Tom is asleep; I can hear his quiet, gentle breathing. It's ages before I'm even drowsy, and I don't sleep before I've done it again, thinking of girls, a girl, any girl. . . Towards dawn, the long-expected thunder rumbles. I surface to heavy, drenching rain, then slide back into

63

sleep and sweet dreams. Next morning is as if the fields, the beach, the rocks are made new; all wet, fresh. There are delicious earth scents, flower scents, though summer blossoms lie battered in mud. The sea is restless.

It is our last day here.

I can't avoid Tom, though that is what I'd like to do; Dad and Aunt Mary – brother and sister – are so close. And she lives nearby. I feel there is something unclean about Tom. I'm cool and off-hand when we talk. But our relationship has existed all our lives and I can't throw it away.

I don't throw it away.

1963

In our twenties we are the best of friends, have no secret from one another, hold back nothing, though we do not meet as often as we did in childhood and adolescence. The pattern of our lives, however, has not been alike, for Tom is a university graduate, has travelled much, and now teaches at a school in London. He is of course unmarried. I left school at eighteen to work in a bank, have rarely been abroad, and in the past twelve years have known many girls. I don't think Tom has the edge on me in sexual experience.

It is the annus mirabilis, or the annus diaboli according to how you look at it – the coldest winter of the century, Profumo's year and Christine Keeler's: Macmillan's government falls; we have the Beatles and endure the Cuba crisis. It's my wedding day. In two months' time President Kennedy will be shot.

The best man is Tom, of course. 'The heterosexual world has all the advantages,' he says as he looks at the presents laid out for the guests' approval – the crockery and cutlery, kitchenware, cruets, linen, towels, bath mats, ash-trays, vases, coffee pots, lampshades, etcetera. 'Nobody blesses *our* liaisons with gifts and celebrations, indeed anything.' (I haven't shown him the dining-room suite, the new car, the bedroom suite.) 'Most people,' he continues, 'try to split us up, not hold us together. We're illegal! A friend of mine was killed in a car crash a fortnight ago; his lover wasn't even invited to the funeral. How is he to be helped with his grief? Which, I may add, is no less genuine than that of any wife or husband.'

'Telling me all this is taking coals to Newcastle. I *know*. The least you have done is to inform me in these matters.'

He grins. 'Thank you for inviting Daryl.'

'Don't be grateful for what is naturally your right!'

Daryl is his lover. They met when Tom was staying at a motel in Cefalu, Sicily. 'I was in bed,' he told me, 'trying to hear the words spoken in the next room. They went on and on, interminably – a man and a woman analysing their relationship, I thought – up and down and roundabout, like a duet in an opera. Then the noises of screwing. Why are motel walls so thin? The number of people I seem to have known intimately over the years in motels! I listen to their voices, their sexual techniques, the cries of their orgasms, but I never meet them, never even *see* them. It's sad! Not on this occasion, however. Their fucking gave me an erection so hard I got out of bed, tiptoed outside wearing only my knickers, and peered through the window. They hadn't drawn the curtains properly, and it wasn't a man and a woman. The bigger man, the one who was doing the fucking, looked up. His face, his body were . . . quite beautiful. He beckoned me inside. If anyone tells you, Chris, that threesomes don't work, they're talking nonsense!'

Threesomes only exist for me in my fantasies, and the other two participants are women. I realise once again that Tom still has the power to shock me. The man who beckoned was Daryl – a long-distance lorry driver. I can't remember the other man's name, but it's not important: his relationship with Daryl ended less than a week after Tom strolled into their lives.

How I met Lynn is a mite more conventional – at the bank's sports club dance. (I play rugby for the bank; scrum half.) The only unconventional aspect of our wedding – and it's so frequent these days that soon it will not be unconventional at all – is Lynn is pregnant. We *have* to marry: both mothers insist. I don't mind. Well . . . I wanted to get married sooner or later. Why not to Lynn? I know no girl more pleasant, more interesting, more attractive. It seems like a good idea. Giving her a baby, however, was not my intention. My record has been spoiled. The pill is not yet universal; condoms, caps, spermicides, and other less than totally satisfactory devices must be used. In the ten years from seventeen to twenty-seven I've not slipped once, but have also not once made love without some contraption or other getting in the way. The heterosexual doesn't have *all* the advantages. 'When a man has his cock inside you,' I said to Tom the evening I told him, 'you don't have to worry you'll end up with a bun in the oven.'

He laughed. 'More's the pity, perhaps.'

'Why?'

'I don't mean I'd like to change sex. No! But I'd like to have children. I'd *love* to be a father, but it will never happen. You *do* have all the advantages!'

Me, a father. Soon now. Will I be able to cope? As I stand in this draughty church, waiting for the organist to strike up the chords of the piece from *Lohengrin*, I glance at Dad. He coped. But I'm not of the same calibre. He's beginning to age now. Retired from work. His hair is pepper and salt. Mum smiles at me, as if to say, 'Have confidence! Believe in yourself; believe in your choice!' I didn't have choice. Did I? Aunt Mary is in the pew behind. This is the first occasion for some years that she and Tom have seen each other. When she discovered what he is, she cut him from her life. 'Are you trying to kill me?' she shouted, and took to her bed for a week. They are both happy, I guess, that they do not meet, don't have to play out some charade of mother-son affection. I think this is terrible.

I catch Daryl's eye. He winks.

Lynn is at the back of the church, a flurry of lace.

1975

How to mark public matters against the events of my existence? There is nothing. The Perons improbably rule Argentina again; Wilson improbably rules England again. But these are facts not worth a passing thought. It is, however, the most momentous year of my life.

Tom, worried about middle age, lifts weights twice a week. I would never have guessed that a specimen so anaemic as he used to be could at thirty-nine become so fit, lean, and youthful. He has urged me to go to a gym too, but I haven't got round to it. I should do something as I no longer play rugby; when I see myself in the bathroom mirror I don't like how I look. My blond hair is thin. I'm paunchy, flabby, and my face has jowls. I wouldn't make a nice young secretary these days fall over backwards. Tom has given up school-teaching. He now lectures at a university, and is a published author. Novels. None of his books has been a great hit, but reviewers say he has 'promise.' He is also big in gay rights – protest rallies, letters to the press; and he has recently taken to plastering himself with badges: I'd feel very awkward if he came into the bank like that. But Lynn has never been uneasy with my homosexual cousin; he often takes her out disco dancing and they have a really good time. I'm too old for that sort of thing. He's still 'married' to Daryl, though it seems to me that they practise gay polygamy rather than anything that resembles the usual heterosexual arrangements.

My marriage is over. It trickled away. Lynn, preoccupied with children, housework, and shopping, has for twelve years bored me to death. Our sex life became a joke. It was never spontaneous, passionate: not once did we do it in the car, on the kitchen floor, upside down on the staircase; not once was I allowed to be in any position other than the missionary. The stories of what Tom tells me he gets up to make me scream with frustration.

I was dying inside. Despite two beautiful children (Graham, nearly twelve, and Alison, ten), a home with every conceivable gadget and comfort, and a good job – I'm now the manager of a bank – there seemed no point, no purpose. It was as if for nearly all my life I had been acting out the role expected of me rather than the one I really wanted. What *did* I want?

I drink too much and I smoke too much.

On the sixteenth of March my horoscope in the newspaper said I would meet a Piscean and begin a wonderful new romance. 'Oh, please!' I said. 'Please! Send her to me! *Any* Piscean will do!' Fate overheard: in a pub that night I met Angie. She is everything I needed sexually and never got – we have done it in the car, on the kitchen floor, upside down on the staircase; it's spontaneous, passionate: totally uninhibited. It has lasted a week, a month, months. Lynn has found out. Inevitably. I couldn't go on lying with conviction about working late, conferences in London, the happiness it was impossible to conceal. She has not taken the news calmly or kindly.

The upshot is that I am in the middle of being divorced. Lynn has the children, the house and almost everything in it. I'm poverty-stricken. I live in two spartan rooms and wonder how I'll ever rake up the deposit on a new house. But I have Angie in bed, all night, every night.

Can I begin a new life at forty? I hope so. Tom says there is no reason why not, then teases me for having put myself into such a bizarre situation in the first place. (He means my marriage to Lynn.) Don't look back, he says. But I am full of remorse. Sick at heart. My parents grieve: they don't understand, though they try. They certainly don't blame Lynn. They see a lot of her, and Tom does too. The children have been staying some weekends with him and Daryl, which makes me jealous – Tom, I begin to think, has the kids he could never have fathered. Graham and Alison like him. The four of them went camping in the Channel Islands last month, and Alison told me they thoroughly enjoyed themselves. I'm not sure I feel happy about my kids intimately observing a life-style such as Tom-and-Daryl's, but it's none of my business now, I suppose. Lynn seems to think it's perfectly all right.

Sometimes I feel utterly depressed, and not even Angie is sufficient recompense. On these occasions I get drunk out of my mind. The only person I could talk to, who would understand what I'm going through, is Aunt Mary. But she doesn't live in England. Four years ago she got married again, to an Australian – and went off with him to settle in Canberra.

My parents still live in the same house: nearly half a century of happy marriage. Though I can now see where the garden ends, the toads still haunt the back of the rockery and the irises still smell of velvet. Red tulip blossom streaks the white cherry petals on the grass. It's good to know there are constants in this bitch of a world.

1984

It's me, Tom, writing the final episode. This entry would be for 1987 if Chris's formula were rigidly stuck to, but in fact it's 1984. Not the year of Orwell's dire predictions, but the year of the great drought. Every weekend this summer Daryl and I have been lying on the beach. Or swimming, surfing, yachting – frequently with Graham and Alison. Alison will be getting married next February: I am to give her away.

Chris died of a heart attack last month. He was never able to survive alone; the day-to-day realities of cooking for himself, fixing his laundry, ironing, or cleaning a house were beyond him. There had always been a woman to do it. Guilt crippled him too. Guilt about Lynn (though in many ways he was glad to be free of a pointless marriage), about his children, who took Lynn's side and who rarely bothered to visit him; guilt that he had broken so totally with convention. The affair with Angie lasted three years, and it was, as he said, intensely physical. For the first time in his life he had found absolute bodily satisfaction: they were fucking, those two, nearly every day, several times a day. His bedroom had huge mirrors on the walls and ceiling, and it contained a great many delightful sexual toys which, after his death, I took away to use in the bedroom I share with Daryl.

Angie grew bored because there was nothing other than sex in the relationship. After she had gone it was downhill the whole way: he drank and smoked himself into his coffin. At forty-eight he was a wreck; fat, bald, shambling, his cheeks a mess of broken capillaries.

Daryl and I have grown very comfortably into each other. We're content. Fulfilled. We are quite domesticated, and love our house with its long, terraced garden that looks out over the sea. We are great gardeners. We have many friends; we travel a lot, and we pub and club on Saturday nights, often with Lynn. AIDS means we no longer practise polygamy (what quaint words Chris used!), but we're not bothered by the loss of that. We're more concerned, obviously, with the illness and death of friends – and of people we've never met. It's appalling. Especially for the young, those who have to grow up with the fact of AIDS. How do men in their twenties, who, finding themselves HIV positive, cope with saying to themselves, 'I've never had a career. I've never had a real lover. And I might die in a year or two'? We never had such problems: maybe, after all, we were born at the luckiest time.

The heterosexual world still has, on the face of it, all the advantages, though gays have moved mountains during my life. To be legal, to be 'out,' to have discos, bars, saunas, to have gay novels and newspapers, to travel on gay holidays, to meet so many other gay people so easily – none of this was possible when I was young. You couldn't, then, be glad; be proud of the difference.

Chris's straightness put him in a straightjacket. When he was freed, he was like a man who has been institutionalised too long – he couldn't cope. But it makes me realise that straights *don't* have all the advantages. Ultimately, gay or straight doesn't matter – it's like cock: it's what you do with it that counts.

WORMS AND GRAVES
AND EPITAPHS

'So there!' said Simon, sticking his tongue out. 'Yaaah!' He raised his hands to his nose and waggled his fingers at her. 'Soppy old Amanda Allgood! Allbad, that's what you are, fat-face!'

'Right, Simple Simon! You'll be sorry for this!' Her cheeks flamed with the annoyance of it. 'You think you're ever so clever, don't you? You're just a horrible little squit, the squittiest little squit in this school.' She looked round to see if it was safe: Miss Lindley was at the other side of the room, bent over Neil Todmarden, trying to show him how to do adverbial clauses. The other kids were shouting and laughing, stuffing paper into ink-wells, scratching names on desk-tops, flicking pellets and banging rulers.

Amanda stood up, crossed the space between the desks, and with a satisfying 'There!' jabbed a compass into Simon's leg. It went in at such an angle that no harm was done; nevertheless he screamed an ear-piercing scream which shocked the class into instant silence.

'Amanda stuck a compass in me!' Simon yelled.

'Amanda, this is the last straw!' Miss Lindley looked worried; the Head, Mr Enever, might appear. 'Go and stand outside at once. *At once!*'

It was Miss Lindley's usual punishment. Sometimes she had such a zest for it that a dozen or more of her pupils found themselves herded together in the corridor. Amanda left the room very slowly, stopping to talk to Rosemary on the way. 'At once, I said!' Miss Lindley shouted, but Amanda stayed to finish her conversation. By the door she muttered something that sounded like 'Silly old cat,' and everyone laughed. Miss Lindley said nothing.

'I'm bleeding!' Simon protested. 'Can I go to the washroom?'

'You stay where you are!' Miss Lindley said. 'If you weren't such an infant these things wouldn't happen in the first place!' She returned to Neil's clauses.

'That's not true!' But there was only a little blood and it didn't really hurt. Simon was soon talking to the boy on his left, Derek Fairey. He didn't much like sitting next to Derek, whose father was the local fishmonger – *Fairey's Fresh Fish* – but nobody else wanted to be with either of them. Derek smelled, if you went too near, of haddock. He was the oldest boy in the class, and the biggest. Simon was the smallest.

'Watch this,' Derek said, and he stood up.

The kids began to snigger and point: Derek was exposing himself. Miss Lindley turned round more quickly than usual, and saw. The kids gasped and fell silent, but another shock was to come, for Derek made no attempt to cover himself; he smiled, and flushed, and seemed pleased that Miss Lindley had noticed.

She was forced into saying something, to *admit* she had noticed. 'What are you doing?' she said, uncertainly, then, the full horror of it dawning on her, she raised her voice: 'Do yourself up at once! How dare you, in front of – of – of the girls to – really, I – I shall tell Mr Enever of this! I shall have you *suspended*, you dirty, disgusting boy!!'

He sat down and did up his flies. The class was absolutely quiet.

'I think it's time you all did some written work,' Miss Lindley said, going back to the teacher's desk. 'Get out your English exercise books, and open *English Made Easy* at page thirty-five. Do the questions on punctuation.'

The only sounds that could be heard in the room now were the rustling of paper and the scratching of pens. It was as if the class realised that things had gone far too far and that, collectively, they had to atone for Derek's behaviour.

'I'm bleeding,' Simon said, again. 'Can I go to the washroom, please?'

Miss Lindley looked at him suspiciously, then said, 'Very well, I suppose so.'

Outside he was surprised to see Amanda: he had forgotten her in the excitement over Derek.

'What's going on? Why's it all so quiet?' She was bubbling with curiosity.

'You stuck a compass in my leg, so why should I tell you?'

'Never mind that now! Tell me what's happened!'

He hit her hard in the stomach with his fist, and ran off to the toilets.

Amanda was absent the following day, but Simon thought nothing of it. Then half-way through English Mr Enever came in, and asked Miss Lindley if she could spare Simon for a few minutes. In his study was a tall, stern man.

'This is Amanda's father,' said Mr Enever.

Simon felt apprehensive. Something weird must have occurred.

'Do you know why she is away?' Mr Enever went on.

'No sir.' Puzzled, he thought: how could I possibly know?

The Headmaster frowned and his bushy eyebrows seemed to join together. The gold-rimmed spectacles made his eyes look fierce and cold. 'Amanda is ill because you hit her in the stomach. It must have been a vicious blow because she was sick as soon as she got home yesterday.'

What lies! Why wasn't she sick at school, then?

'I hope you aren't going to deny it, for that will only make things worse for you. It obviously is true, otherwise Mr Allgood wouldn't be here, would he?'

'No sir. I –'

'I warn you not to tell any lies!'

73

'No sir.' Standing between these two towering men he was insignificant and helpless. Perhaps it was just possible they were right. Could two such severe men be wrong? It might be best to accept what they said; it was dangerous to argue with adults. Sometimes, even, they were pleased if you agreed with them that you had erred, although it could well be another kid's fault. Simon's experience in the past had proved it was always safer to say what adults wanted to hear.

'Hitting defenceless girls is a serious matter,' Mr Enever went on. 'I hope you're well and truly ashamed of yourself. Are you?'

'Yes sir.' Defenceless! Amanda was about as defenceless as an army tank!

'Mr Allgood wants to punish you himself. He wants to cane you. Is that fair?'

Simon shivered. It was terrifying, the results of actions done in fun or without thinking. There was scarcely any step you could take that avoided collision with the power adults wielded. A strange man could walk into the school, judge him, and be given the right to thrash him, all in a few seconds. Next door in Miss Lindley's room – it seemed light-years away – the happy noise of pandemonium rose to fresh peaks and died.

'However, I think it might cause unnecessary complications,' Mr Enever said, vaguely. 'So Mr Allgood and I have decided that you should report to his house on Saturday morning and do two hours' useful work. He wants a fence creosoted, and there are some brass ornaments to clean. If you fail to turn up I shall cane you myself on Monday. Is that clear?'

'Yes sir.'

'Are we being fair? Are we being lenient?'

'Oh, yes sir.'

'You can count yourself lucky. If Mr Allgood had had his way you'd have had six strokes of the cane from him, and I daresay it would hurt. Before you go home this afternoon you'll write to Amanda and apologize, and I shall want to read the letter when you've finished. Now go back to your class.'

Simon glanced up at Mr Allgood. It was impossible to tell if he was appeased or not.

Simon and Derek were sitting in the headquarters of the Fernleaf Gang in the disused, overgrown cemetery in Grange Road. Last year Richard had found a hole in the railings just big enough to squeeze through, and since then the Gang had held their meetings in this dense clump of bushes in the middle of the cemetery, a perfect hide-out. Branches were interwoven so thickly here that the only way to get in was by crawling flat against the ground. But it was worth the effort, for the inside was an airy tent full of green shadows, the walls of which were twigs and leaves. If the Gang discovered Simon and Derek there would be trouble, for they were not members. Simon had been told about the headquarters by his cousin Allan, who made him swear on pain of excruciating punishments not to reveal the secret to a living soul. But since yesterday Derek seemed more important and more interesting than the Fernleafs, so Simon had blurted out the information. What did it matter? Derek would protect him.

'I don't understand it,' Derek said for the third time. 'Of course she's telling a load of lies, so why didn't you say so?'

'I was so frightened I didn't know what to say.'

'What are you going to do about it?' He was whittling at a stick, sharpening its point with a penknife.

'I don't know. Nothing.'

'I'll help you. I'll hold her down, then you can bash her good and proper.'

'That's no use.'

'Well, I wouldn't do two hours' work for him. On a Saturday morning! Why don't you tell your Dad?'

'I haven't got a Dad.'

'My Dad wouldn't make me do it. You're crazy not protesting.'

Simon looked out between the branches. At his feet runners of bindweed wound round twigs that sagged too near the ground, pegging them fast; just beyond, wild poppies made small scarlet circles deep in the jungle of couch-grass that was choking them. Everything stretched upwards for light. Above, in the freedom of the air, the summer afternoon sun was already beginning to slant, and insects in the shafts of light that reached down through gaps between trees looped and spun in gold whirls. The sky was pale, almost silky.

'Why don't you answer?'

'It's no use. Mr Allgood would be up on Monday, and then I'd get six.'

'I think you're a coward, Simon. A stinking old coward.'

Simon tried to divert the conversation. 'Did Miss Lindley report you?' he asked.

'What for?'

'You know.' He giggled.

'Oh.' Derek seemed embarrassed. 'Of course not,' he said. 'Do you think she's going to let Enever realise she's so bad at keeping order that I dared to do that?'

Plucking up courage, Simon said, 'Show us again.' Derek did not move. 'It's. . .' Simon faltered, blushing. Derek frowned and concentrated on carving lumps out of his stick.

'I only did it for a bet,' he muttered.

'Please,' Simon urged.

'No!' He threw down the stick and snapped his knife shut. 'No! Why should I?' He stood up, suddenly dangerous. 'You want us to play about, don't you? You're dirty.' He looked at Simon a moment, uncertain. Then he began to push through the branches into the sunlight, trampling a new path, out of the headquarters. 'You're dirty,' he repeated, pulling the briars off his clothes. His sleeve ripped and he swore as a stone stubbed his foot; then he disappeared, submerged in lilac and hazel and honeysuckle. There were swishing sounds as his legs swathed through the tangle of undergrowth, the crack of twigs, the startled twitter of a bird flying up through the trees. Soon all was still.

Perhaps Derek was right, Simon thought; perhaps it was dirty. Was exposing it at school something different then, a triumph of daring and courage? He didn't know the answer to that. What he did know was that he wanted to put his hands round it and – and for Derek to do the same to him.

Here lies Thomas Ebenezer Peckham, died August 14th 1844, aged 72 years. And Enoch walked with God and he was not, for God took him. Charlotte Emily, wife of the above, died May 18th 1860, aged 80 years.

> Servant of Christ, well done,
> Rest from thy loved employ;
> The Battle fought, the Victory won,
> Enter thy Master's joy.

It was one of the few tombstones that was still legible. Its message disturbed Simon; it was so sure in tone. How did these people know they would be in Heaven? Other inscriptions nearby had been obliterated. Moss grew in the line of letters, or black streaks like long dark tears wept by giant eyes smudged out names and dates. Odd details remained, like the sculptor's signature, Brackley of Chelton, in a bottom right-hand corner, meant to be unobtrusive; or Augusta Sarah who expired on, and the rest was smeared out by a green stain. The optimism of the texts was repeated wherever he could see the words: 'There shall be no night there.' 'There is therefore no condemnation to them which are in Christ Jesus.' 'Lead kindly light amid the encircling gloom; lead thou me on.' 'Thou shalt come to thy grave in a full age as a shock of corn cometh in in his season.'

Here were children, wives, husbands, whole families: a justice of the peace born in Suffolk, whose relics since 1886 had been in a vast marble box at the top of a flight of steps; the two Howard children, one dead at five weeks, the second at five months, under an imposing stone monument more than twice as big as they were; a boy of thirteen, also named Simon, whom the Lord had called to His Bosom on Christmas Eve, 1902. What was it like to be that Simon? He imagined himself a fleshless grinning skeleton in a shroud, the bones of his hands clasped in prayer on the rib-cage of his chest – as bishops and knights lie on tombs in cathedrals. There was earth, damp, worms, an eternity of staring upwards; nothing else. It was a good state to be, this nothing, he thought; there would no longer be any blame or accusing fingers. Being Simon wouldn't even be a worry any more.

The cemetery was a very private, enclosed world. It had been derelict for half a century: bindweed and ivy climbed up the tombs; crosses and angels lay prostrate; urns were scattered in pieces – one, on the Howard tomb, was like an unfinished sculpture of a wild beast ready to spring out of the stone, snarling and tearing. There were rows of important and fussy monuments crowded together, pining up towards the sun. Buttercups, meadowsweet, bluebells, stinging nettles and all kinds of grasses strangled them, and the statues and plinths tottered and lurched under the pressure. Soon they would all fall over, and the immense profusion of weeds would obliterate them entirely.

Back in the headquarters Simon stretched out on the ground. No point in going home yet; his mother would not be in till six. A bumblebee blundered through the leafy roof above him; it wheeled round and round in half a dozen uncertain circles, its hum a deeper bass than an ordinary honeybee. It swerved towards him, then it swayed through an opening in the branches and was gone. In the distance a blackbird sang, a sound like a stream filtering through pebbles. The late afternoon light glanced through in long splinters; glinting on a rhododendron's hard dark evergreen as if it was water. Looking up at the undersides of yellow-green lime leaves, Simon could distinguish the pattern of veins, the thin, living skeleton.

He was almost asleep. A mosquito droned near him, insistent; it tickled his forehead as it settled. Smack: it was dead. Dust in the air, the pollen from blossoms, made him sneeze. Far away an aeroplane whined. He imagined he was in it, over a sea of thick cotton-wool clouds. In the real sea beneath was an iceberg; it was visible, white and frosty, through a hole in the cotton wool. The other seven eighths of it under the ocean was clear, like blue glass. He slept.

He dreamed that the cemetery was burning. The fire crept nearer, crackling and rustling in the undergrowth, until the smoke made him cough. He opened his eyes. He was looking up at the unsmiling faces of the Fernleaf boys – Neil, Ivor, Richard, and his cousin Allan.

'What are you doing in here?' Neil demanded.

Simon blinked. To say 'just sleeping' sounded stupid.

'Don't you know that this is private property?' said Richard.

The boys stared down at him: he did not expect them to be merciful. He was lying on his back, an easy target; they towered over him as Mr Enever and Mr Allgood had done. He appealed to his cousin: 'Allan!' But Allan moved away; a speck in one eye suddenly troubled him.

'This is our hide-out,' said Neil. 'You're trespassing, see? We're going to teach you a lesson so you won't come in here again.' He turned to the others. 'Is he guilty?' Neil was the worst of them, mean and tough, with a vicious temper.

'Guilty,' said Richard, and Ivor echoed him. Allan rubbed an eye, and flicked the shock of fair hair back off his forehead.

'Grab him!' Neil shouted, and he dived on Simon's legs. Simon thrashed out, but Richard held his arms in a tight grip; Ivor pulled off his blazer and he heard pencils fall out of his pocket onto the ground. 'Mind my things!' he yelled. 'Allan! Help me!' But Allan's hands were tearing at his shirt, and, too late, he realised what they intended to do: one sharp tug and the shirt was off, a button flying through the air, then his vest was pulled over his head and fingers were undoing the clasp of his belt, undoing the zip; several more violent wrenches and his trousers, underwear, socks and shoes were dragged off his legs and feet. The boys let go. They stood round him, panting, flushed, silent. Allan was holding the shirt.

Simon's face was hot with shame. The thin, nude body which eight eyes stared at was, he guessed, a pitiful sight. It shouldn't exist: that's what they were thinking, he said to himself. It shouldn't exist. All the bones seemed to

79

protrude through the skin; the ribs were like a xylophone; there were hardly any muscles on the arms at all. Between his legs dangled a pathetic little worm.

Allan dropped the shirt and walked away.

'Feeble little squit,' said Neil. He threw the trousers and the shoes high into the bushes.

'C'm'on,' said Richard, with a jerk of his head. They crawled out under the branches. Simon listened to their laughter as they struggled through the undergrowth; the silence, when he could hear them no more, pressed in on him. The leaves above seemed to move nearer, almost wrapped themselves round him like a winding-sheet. The silence, the closed-in space: he was a nothing, in a coffin. The skinny legs and arms ceased to be him. Nothing existed any longer: no more hot bodies hurt him; no adults accused. He was invisible, just the spirit of the place, as remote from contact as a fly in the centre of an iceberg.

'I saw all that,' someone said. Derek.

Simon jumped in fright, and, realising he was still naked, covered himself with his shirt.

'I watched it all from behind that tree,' Derek went on.

'Why didn't you help me, then?' Simon said. 'Go away!'

'I've changed my mind.'

'About what?'

In answer, Derek opened his flies, and pulled it out. It was very stiff. 'Put one of your hands on it,' he said. Simon obeyed. 'Now move your hand up and down. Yes! Like that . . . but slower . . . slow is best. Lovely! Shall I do it to you?'

'Yes. Yes, please!'

'Trust in the Lord.' 'O taste and see how sweet is the Lord.' 'And though worms destroy this body, yet in my flesh shall I see God.' Then there was a square of land without even an outline of a grave, so dense was the hawthorn and ivy, old man's beard and blackberry. After this a cluster of unassuming ordinary tombstones huddled together as if for shelter, like sheep on the lee side of a field. One ancient inscription, to Annie Phillips of Laurel House, said

The place of John I covet
More than a Seraph's throne:
Then I'll see my Beloved,
And heave my final Groan.

Next to it was Captain Ezekiel Percy Lindley, drowned off the Cape of Good Hope, 'Perished as though he had never been.' It was just a plaque; there was no grave.

He walked on, thinking about himself in the third person, imagining he was dead. 'Mr Allgood, Mr Enever and the Fernleaf boys seemed to believe there was something wrong with him, that he was like some kind of sucker growth. Mr Allgood demanded that he should spend Saturday morning creosoting a fence and polishing brass ornaments. He refused.'

Yes, he would refuse to go. It didn't matter what happened as a result; he could take six stinging blows on his bum. He sniffed his hands: they smelled faintly of haddock. As he squeezed through the railings he wondered which part of the cemetery he would like to be buried in. Over there, he decided: it was near a chestnut tree now in full bloom, its white spires a little town of wigwams. What epitaph would he have on his gravestone? None at all, probably. As he turned into his street he saw his mother anxiously looking for him. On Saturday he would not go to Mr Allgood's; he would lie in bed till late, then, after breakfast, meet Derek in another part of the cemetery far away from the Fernleafs' hide-out. His worm wasn't so pathetic, he decided. He would touch and be touched, rub his hand up and down Derek's, have Derek's hand do the same to his, and thoroughly enjoy both the sensation of this form of exercise and the gorgeous pleasure of the end-product's arrival.

MENDOCINO IN OCTOBER

It was Angus's fifth time here, but his first without a lover. He had always been fond of someone, and could not exist properly without loving. He had loved his parents, and his English teacher at high school, then, at university, a series of blond jocks; but none of them had really reciprocated his feelings. He was a gentle, compassionate man, still, in his forties, good-looking in a battered sort of way, and ready to give anything; a man who made others think, well, why not? He'll *do*.

Mendocino. Mendocino! He had always considered it the ideal place to be with a lover. A honeymoon retreat. Even with Vivian, his oldest friend, it had its customary enchantment. A small town of clapboard houses and a wooden church reminiscent of New England, on a rugged cape defying the Pacific Ocean. October now, the sunlight golden, a few wisps of fog in the pines. The garden blossom was still a blaze of Indian summer – cornflowers, petunias, pelargoniums, black-eyed susans, marigolds. Marigold: the colour of October. The colour of Mendocino.

They were staying at the motel on the cliffs where he had always stayed, where he'd brought at one time or another each of the four men who had shared his adult life; Mario, Rick, Pat, Lonny. A row of wind-wrecked

Monterey cypresses sheltered it from the ocean. Last night was so warm he and Vivian had sat under the trees till half past twelve, gazing at the black water below and the lines of white tossing surf that broke the darkness. They had listened, in the pauses of their conversation (which was about love and loving – all feigning and folly, they agreed) to the churning of the sea. Its restlessness, they said, its flux, was a metaphor for their lives, and they quoted bits of *Dover Beach* aloud –

> Its melancholy, long, withdrawing roar,
> Retreating to the breath
> Of the night-wind, down the vast edges drear
> And naked shingles of the world.

They drank brandy from paper cups, and they didn't go to bed till the bottle was finished.

Now, over an excellent brunch on the terrace of Thar She Blows! they were reading the papers and watching the people go by. Mendocino had always attracted oddities; upper-class bag ladies in ponchos and ethnic sandals, middle-aged hippies who felt even Berkeley too conservative, oddball men and women frantically searching for spiritual repair and inner peace through messages, meditation, and mantras.

'Listen to this,' Vivian said. She was reading the local paper, *Mendocino Country*.

'The calendar of events?'

'Yes. "Redwood Valley. Ongoing Group Rebirthing Class. Experience Transformational Breathwork in the context of a master rebirther and group energy." What does it *mean*?'

Angus laughed. 'What else?'

'"Forestville. A week-long educational vacation with the staff of the California School of Herbal Studies. Medicinal herbology, herbal first-aid, flower essences, preparation, formulas, psychic attunement with plants."'

'In other words – "I think that I shall never see A poem lovely as a tree."'

'The cost of that one is *three hundred dollars*! Jesus H. *Christ!*'

His first visit here had been with Mario. They had met in a bar on Polk, and when they saw each other naked that night they both said they had never before seen such beauty. A week passed, and they said they loved each other. A month passed, and they were living together in a flat on Eureka Street. At first it was all worship. Adoration. Mario was a ballet dancer, which Angus thought a very exciting thing to be. His own nine-to-five office job (health scheme, pension, six weeks vacation a year) seemed dull in comparison. He loved his other half being a dancer. He loved Mario *because* he was a dancer. Mario's friends were now his friends; he became quite expert on classical ballet, was very much at home in conversations about entrechats, arabesques, pas de deux; knew what Ashton or Balanchine or Tudor had choreographed for whom and when and where; could discuss easily the sleeping arrangements of the world of dance – whose lover was new, who had suddenly left, who had unexpectedly returned.

There were problems, however. Mario wasn't easy to live with. He was moody, occasionally violent – he would throw his dinner at Angus when he was in a temper, or smash up the crockery – and not always honest. Sometimes he was unfaithful. Angus took all this in his stride; he forgave Mario, always turning the other cheek. It was a part of loving, he told himself. He had made a commitment, and nothing would change that.

It endured seven years, quite extraordinarily long, friends said afterwards. Mario, tired of Angus's gentle nature, the domesticity and the devotion, left him for good one Christmas Eve. There was no other man involved. He just didn't want Angus. Angus, alone, couldn't sleep properly for months. He even thought of suicide. It took him a year to recover – which is about par for the course. 'My world has collapsed,' he said, again and again, to anyone who cared to listen. He left Eureka Street the following Christmas and moved into a studio in Noe Valley. A few days later he met Rick, an event which completed his recovery.

In Mendocino Angus and Mario stayed in room number one at the motel. That weekend, another golden fall, they drank a lot, ate good dinners, walked for miles on the beaches and in the forest, screwed ecstatically, and said how much they loved each other: their relationship would last all their lives.

'How about this!' Vivian said. '"Ukiah. A Polarity class is scheduled at the Wellness School of Holistic Health. Polarity is a form of massage which uses the hands as a pair of magnets to create a flow of energy to relieve pain and dysfunction in the body, facilitating optimal health."'

'Hmmm.'

'You're not listening.'

'I am.'

'O.K.' She laughed. 'Try this one, then. "The Tub Club. We have a new shipment of antique silk kimonos plus Tibetan tankas and expanded New Age music selection. Also unique style, hand-fabricated wind-bells with three distinct tones; guaranteed to rust."'

'I like that!'

Guaranteed to rust. Rick was not as cute as Mario. His body was a little too hairy for Angus's taste, and he frequently took hours to come, or he didn't come at all, which left Angus dissatisfied, however good his own orgasm had been. He looked for blame only in himself; what was he doing wrong? Did a feeling of this-is-not-as-wonderful-as-Mario somehow communicate itself to Rick? Not that he ever, in word or deed, hinted that it was this side of paradise. He loved Rick, was committed, had promised. There were no domestic problems as there had been with Mario. Rick wasn't moody or bad-tempered, and never unfaithful. The studio in Noe Valley was a haven of peace. Rick was a journalist, and again Angus found this an exciting profession; it was one of the reasons why he loved Rick. Rick's friends became his friends, glamorous people who talked of deadlines, assignments and exclusives; Angus could now tell others what Herb Caen had not put in his column, which sub-editor had subbed what, which editor had edited whom; and he could laugh or express surprise or be knowing about yet another world where people's sleeping arrangements were rarely settled or unremarkable. Angus had no world of his own, and if anyone had ever suggested (which they didn't) that he ought to have one, he would have been profoundly astonished. Love, he'd have said, was putting another's interests first, seeking *his* happiness.

The problem was Rick was English. He was only in San Francisco for a year. At the beginning this didn't seem to matter – he could probably stay another year, even two; a marriage could be arranged so he'd get citizenship; Angus, if all else failed, could go on to part-time work (with part-time salary, of course) and live each September to February in London. This sacrifice of his career was of no importance; love came first. But as the weeks rolled on, Rick began to think of many good reasons why Angus should not ruin his career, why marriages were impossible to arrange; and his newspaper, he said, wouldn't allow him another year abroad. The San Franciscan they'd got in his place was eager to return to San Francisco.

Their weekend in Mendocino, in room nine at the motel, was spoiled by the imminence of Rick's departure. Their only attempt at love-making was disastrous, and Angus thought of what it had been like here with Mario.

Farewells on Oakland Station were tearful. (Rick was crossing the continent by train and flying home from New York; he wanted, he said, to 'see America.') Angus did not know it then, but twenty minutes later Rick was chatting to an extremely pretty youth who was travelling from San Jose to Chicago; this led to sex in the California Zephyr's geriatric loo, where Rick experienced no problem with orgasm, absolutely no problem at all. Angus heard about it months afterwards – the gay world, for gossip, being like a global family – from a friend of a friend of a friend of a friend.

'Shall we take a walk?' Vivian suggested.

They looked at more gardens; busy lizzies, chrysanthemums, dahlias, pyracantha laden with dazzling red berries, maples letting bright souvenirs of autumn float to the ground. Out at sea a foghorn boomed. The little church reminded Angus of Bergman: that bleak, cold

86

film, *Winter Light*; yes, there was in the clean simplicity of its structure something Scandinavian. Parked cars had stickers that said, 'Nuclear Weapons – may they rust in peace.' They went into shops – Temptations, Pentacles, Personal Expressions – and looked at a bewildering variety of expensive junk and knick-knackery – garlic crushers, boxed votive candles, quilted pot-holders, fragrant spice trivets, simmering potpourris, stained glass shamrocks. Outside the Jungian Dream Institute they read the posters: 'Trance Dance Workshop, with chanting and percussion. Become at ease receiving and focusing healing trance energy in a spirit of fun and seriousness. Bring a blanket and knee pads' – 'For sale – mural, sixteen feet by eighteen feet. Abstract, in black and white housepaint on mahogany plywood. Can be viewed at the Alternative Art Space.' The Alternative Art Space, they discovered, was the local synonym for the used book store.

'This is an insane community,' Angus said.

Vivian agreed. 'But one of the most beautiful corners on God's earth.'

They read the menu outside the Seagull Inn, and decided to eat there; it looked good and reasonably priced. She ordered oysters and chicken kiev, he shrimp louie and beef bourguignon. They drank an excellent local wine.

He had eaten here on his third visit, with Pat; they had come up with three friends, Joe and Stephen, who were lovers, and Sean. They all stayed in room fifteen at the motel, which had two king-size double beds.

A year had passed, the statutory time, since Rick went; Angus had left the studio in Noe Valley and was now installed in an apartment on Haight. He met Pat the day he buried his mother, and was very surprised, considering the emotional traumas of the funeral and trying to comfort his dad before, during, and after, that he was able to screw so successfully. He was more than ready, again, to love, and, for a while, he did. But Pat was an insensitive man; there were no nuances in his thinking or feeling. He moved in with Angus because the fucking was good, and Angus was mild, easy-going, and friendly. He was quite unable to meet Angus's needs – yes, Angus surprised himself by discovering, at last, that he had needs of his own – but that didn't cause problems. Sacrifice, he still thought, was a part of loving. The real problems were that Pat was absolutely incapable of telling the truth, and wanted to sleep with a great many other men. It took only four months for Angus to conclude that love had either died or had never been there to begin with, and that he, for the first time in his life, could break promises, welch on commitments. It was a shock realising this; an amazement, a revelation. He felt he had grown older, or, at least, grown up; he experienced – and cautiously permitted himself to enjoy – a new, heady whiff of freedom. He would leave Pat one day: it would not this time be the other way round.

But three years passed before he did so. He should have left at once, but, he reasoned, the sex was the best he'd ever had; why abandon that and possibly get nothing in exchange? He hated living alone, eating alone, sleeping alone. He had to be with somebody! In bed he and Pat did everything he'd thought about doing and never done, and often they did it with one, two, three, or four others joining in.

Pat was a stockbroker, and, as usual, Angus found himself involved with a new set of friends. He read the business pages of *The San Francisco Chronicle* now, and learned about the rise and fall of prices, currency fluctuations, bonds, shares, securities, dividends, loans. He was at ease with the jargon – bears, bulls, corrections, crashes, rallies and so on; and even risked a little money of his own occasionally. And behind all the financial transactions, indeed sometimes influencing them, there was discreet and indiscreet coupling as varied and unpredictable as the mating of dancers or journalists.

On the king-size beds in Mendocino, Angus and Pat romped with Joe, Stephen, and Sean, à deux, à trois, à quatre, à cinq. After three days everybody had been in and out of everybody else. Watching, as he rested alone on one of the beds, the other four hard at it on the other bed, Angus took a photograph. He had it still: two pairs of well-rounded buns and eight assorted hairy thighs, but it

88

was impossible at this distance in time to know what bits belonged to whom. It was all very silly, he said to himself, and very seventies. It had, unfortunately, happened during the early eighties.

Their meal finished, Angus and Vivian sipped green chartreuse, and were aware, in this ultra health-conscious town, of a few raised eyebrows when they both lit cigars. Vivian reopened *Mendocino Country*. '"Body Freedom Sensuality Workshop",' she read. '"Cast off limiting societal belief patterns about sexuality. Learn what it means to be spiritual beings in physical bodies. Tantra, deep sharing, and meditation guided by special guest.' Sounds like a wife-swopping coven. Perhaps, in these parts, one should say *person*-swopping coven.'

Angus did not reply.

'"Teresa Sproat, grand piano, live in concert at the Arena Theatre, eight p.m. A range of music from Mac-Dowell and Field to Moeran and Rubbra. Sproat travels the world playing in small towns and schools where piano concerts are seldom heard." Because where they are often heard people would rather listen to somebody else? What's wrong?'

'I'm thinking.'

'Of what?'

'Lesions.'

She stretched out a hand and touched his face. 'They aren't visible,' she said.

'Not that kind of lesion. The ones men cause.'

He left Pat for Lonnie; this time it was the Real Thing. They loved each other – so Angus thought – with heart and mind and soul and body. They fulfilled each other's every possible need and desire as friend, father, mother, brother, son, teacher, pupil, travel companion, sex object, lover. Angus found total happiness in roles he didn't know, previously, he could play, or that he wished for; he hadn't realised for instance that he could be a father figure, or how consoling it was that a man could be maternal in all the ways his own mother had refused to be. Inevitably, with a change of lover, came a change of living quarters. This time he rented half a duplex on

Diamond Heights, which, when the fog allowed, had a magical view of the city. The cocktail hour on the deck, enjoying the view and the view of each other, was, they agreed, more than this side of paradise. Angus paid the rent, indeed paid for everything, which had not happened in his other relationships – those affairs had been on a strictly half each understanding. Lonnie was unemployed. Angus did not at all mind this doubling of his expenditure; it was a part of loving. Nor did he mind that there was no career to learn. It was silly, he had long since decided, to have been a dance enthusiast, a newspaper hanger-on, a business groupie. He had friends of his own to introduce to Lonnie, who – it was the one fly in the ointment – seemed to have reservations about this new lover. These friends thought, but they did not say it till afterwards, that Lonnie was a selfish little shit who was merely interested in the pleasures that derived from Angus's cock and cheque book.

Angus ignored the warning signals: the doubts of friends; that Lonnie, in bed, was only into himself ('Suck my right nipple . . . now suck my cock . . . kiss me . . . don't get inside me just yet'); that conversations with Lonnie were mostly about Lonnie; that Lonnie spent too much time with his former lover – 'I don't want to throw away a very important friendship.'

Mendocino with Lonnie, in motel room number three, was of course the ultimate in romantic bliss.

Pat called one evening; he needed to see Angus as soon as possible. It really was urgent. They met for a drink: Pat had taken an AIDS test and was HIV positive.

Angus, feeling once again that his world had collapsed, told Lonnie. If he and Lonnie were carrying the virus, he reasoned, they really would be together always; no other man, nothing could possibly come between them; they would comfort each other, nurse each other, love each other till death did them part. They decided to take the test. And were both positive.

Lonnie freaked out completely. He fled from Angus as he might a leper, and returned to his previous lover. Pat, soon afterwards, met a man he was still living with, and did not tell him he had the virus. Lonnie at least did tell the previous lover, who was so glad to have him back he didn't mind if their sex life was unsafe. Lonnie thought this the ultimate in nobility.

Angus, moving into a house on Dolores, thought it the ultimate in crass stupidity. 'Why do I without fail choose such absolute jerks for lovers?' he asked.

Vivian stopped reading *Mendocino Country*, thought for a moment, then said, 'That's too complex for any answer I could give. I don't even know if it's the right question. You have to say to yourself . . . that in all these things there's a large amount of luck . . . good or bad as it may turn out to be. You have to accept, particularly at the beginning, so much in good faith. Be guided by intuition.'

'I have too much faith. And no intuition.'

'You do seem to have a big flashing light on your head that says "Sucker!" Pat with his ferrety looks . . . and Rick was so *damp*. Mario . . . a nice man, but I'd never have gotten involved with someone that unstable. As for Lonnie. . .' She sighed. 'How are you? I mean . . . the. . .'

'I'm all right.'

He had Kaposi's sarcoma. The disfiguring lesions had begun to appear on his legs and back nine months ago. They had spread now to his neck and face, but it was possible, still, to hide them from public view with the help of make-up. It was as if some alien being, some evil, monstrous thing was inexorably growing into his body, as in *The Quatermass Experiment*. He had, it was reckoned, about a year to live.

He, who had only existed to love, now had no lover. And all those former lovers of his were settled and content: the friend of the friend of the friend of the friend who'd told him of Rick's escapade on the train reported that Rick had been living with someone for nearly five years; and Mario, whom Angus saw occasionally, had grown up – was not so neurotic nor so restless, was more inclined to choose domestic peace, had become like Angus – and lived with a man as moody and self-centred as he had once been.

Pat and Lonnie had no symptoms of AIDS.

It was unfair: it was fucking unjust.

Next day, their last in Mendocino, Angus and Vivian sunbathed on the beach and walked along the cliffs. The weather was still golden October: perfection. The fog – sombre November – tried at times to intrude, but was beaten back by the warmth. The sea, calmer than yesterday, slid and whispered, wrinkled and murmured to itself, was green, then blue, then turquoise; the occasional line of surf without power now, a scratch on glass. The sea-weed rose and fell: it looked like fields of brown bulbs with enormous stems, or patches of gigantic beetroots; uncovered on rocks it resembled dwarf palm forests. Gulls complained. Otters gambolled. Pelicans drifted.

They talked a great deal about friendship; friends, they agreed, were far superior to lovers any day of the week. Angus and Vivian had always been true to one another. There had not been at any time so much as a hint of betrayal.

Suddenly, an astonishing thing far out at sea – huge creatures, leviathans, leaping and plunging, spouting water: a school of whales heading south. The world is mysterious and beautiful, Angus said to himself. We are not upon a darkling plain where ignorant armies clash by night. He was happy. Joyous.

Vivian, staring at the ocean, said, 'I've never seen that before! I'll remember it as long as I live!'

'So will I.' He laughed: unrancorously.

They talked for a while about death. 'I'll be with you,' she said. 'When it. . .'

'I shan't come to Mendocino, ever again.'

'No. Nor will I.'

He sobbed a little. She held him, and kissed him. He felt only a calm acceptance of . . . everything.

That night, waking at four thirty, he wondered for a moment where he was. Then he heard Vivian's quiet, even breathing in the other bed, and, outside, the roar of the sea. He did not know why, but he was profoundly comforted, and slept again.

SWEATERS

For Jim Palmer

In no other city they'd visited, Tim said to Colin, had so many strangers come up to them and talked. And these people spoke such good English! It never occurred in Florence, Seville, Geneva. Sometimes it was because the stranger realised the pair of them were chattering in English; sometimes it was the look of their Western clothes. The conversation invariably started thus: did they want to buy any roubles? Two for a pound was the standard offer, but it could be three, even four. (The official exchange rate was one for one.) No, they didn't want to buy any roubles. They had more than they needed, and it was difficult to find a way of spending them in this city that curiously despised its own currency, that was much more interested in obtaining dollars, pounds, francs, marks. Then . . . maybe they wanted to sell some of their clothes? Twenty roubles for Tim's sweater. Thirty for Colin's jacket. No, they replied. No, no, no! It was annoying.

On one occasion, however, this racketeering turned out to be useful. Seats for the opera and the ballet were unobtainable: 'Sold out,' they were told at the Kirov box office. But they acquired tickets for *Aida* (in Russian) and *The Sleeping Beauty* from a street person, in exchange for some blank videotapes that could only be bought in tourist shops, ones that Leningraders were not allowed to enter. 'It's like *Alice in Wonderland*,' Colin said.

The young man now staring at him – very cute – was not, he thought, interested in a currency fiddle. Not this time. Colin was waiting for Tim in a subway that led down to the Metro: Tim had dashed back to the hotel for his umbrella; it looked as if it might rain, he said. Colin said rain was very unlikely, but Tim had gone, nevertheless.

The young man smiled, and Colin smiled in acknowledgment. A second youth came up to the first, greeted him, and in answer to something said, pointed questioningly at Colin. The first young man then made his intentions daringly obvious by placing both his hands on his crotch, and he gestured, as if masturbating. Colin's eyes widened: in London he'd have had few qualms, but this was Russia; and despite Gorbachev and detente the Soviets still had Siberia and the secret police. But, after a moment, he nodded his head and imitated the young man's gesture.

They were separated for a while by a stream of Leningraders flowing out of the station, a crowd like any crowd one might see in any big city disgorging from the underground at this time of day – workers hurrying home, lost in their own thoughts, faces glazed.

Tim arrived. 'I think I'm being cruised,' Colin said.

'Good Lord. Where? Which one?'

The crowd had dwindled, and Colin was able to point him out.

'*Both* of them, Coll-doll?'

'The guy on the left.'

'The good-looking one.'

Colin laughed. 'Naturally!'

'Shall I make myself scarce for a bit?'

'Well . . . it could be interesting to see what occurs.'

'I'll stay here with my copy of *Pravda*. I enjoy trying to figure out the letters of the alphabet. I won't vanish . . . just in case. Go and talk to them.'

'Just in case of what?'

'The K.G.B.'

As he approached the two Russians, the second boy walked off; Colin paused to see where he went. Aha! He was going to speak to Tim.

94

Konstantin, age twenty, a student. He was supposed to be at a lecture right now, but he was so bored with the subject – Marxism-Leninism – that he couldn't be bothered to go. 'There's too much Lenin in Russia,' he said. 'It's Lenin, Lenin, Lenin all the time!' He had wavy brown hair, dark eyes, and a thin ikon-like face with prominent cheek-bones; a type Colin and Tim, on many occasions since they flew into Leningrad a week ago, had thought extremely attractive. 'Have a Lenin badge,' Konstantin said with a laugh, and he gave Colin a cheap tie-pin which had on it a portrait of the great man in profile. He longed to escape to the West, he said, to travel, to be free, to be himself; here – he sounded nervous – he was . . . illegal. 'Do you know somewhere we could go?'

Back to the hotel? Konstantin would not have the necessary pass to enter, and though the doorman more often than not didn't ask guests for identification, a Russian might have to be smuggled in. It was too risky. 'I'm afraid I don't,' Colin said.

'There's a park quite near here.'

'Is it safe?'

'More or less.'

'But . . . what about our friends? We can't just leave them.'

'I told Yuri to follow . . . to keep an eye open. Just in case.'

It was many years since Colin had had sex so furtively – in the bushes in a park, jeans and knickers round his ankles, the rest of his clothes still on, and looking over his shoulder every so often when he thought he heard someone nearby. But Konstantin had a slim, smooth boy's body, and kissed so passionately, was so turned on, that Colin thought it must be ages since he had last had a man.

East-West relations, he said to himself as they came. Glasnost.

They held each other, tenderly. 'I wish we were indoors . . . and fucking,' Konstantin said. Then, after a while, 'Have you any condoms I could buy?'

Not sweaters. Not roubles for pounds. Condoms. 'I have a few in my room at the hotel,' he answered. 'Can't you get them in Russia?'

'Oh, yes. But we think the Western brands are more reliable.'

Colin laughed. 'I'll give you some. But first . . . we ought to find Tim and Yuri.'

They were not far away, talking on a seat by a flowerbed of daffodils, and smoking cigarettes. 'You've both got mud on your knees,' Tim said. A bit crossly, Colin thought.

Yuri shivered. 'The nights are still cold,' he said. 'Please sell me your sweater, Tim.'

'He's done nothing but beg for my sweater,' Tim murmured. 'Can't talk about anything else. He'd give me twenty roubles. Forty roubles. Forty roubles and his body. I don't want his roubles. And I certainly don't want his body! Whining . . . like a bitch on heat!'

'You want Konstantin's body?'

'Was it good?'

Colin did not reply to that. 'Sell him your sweater,' he said.

'Are you mad?'

'Go on. Sell him your sweater.'

'All . . . right.' He turned to Yuri, and said, as if he had just made up his mind about something he'd been contemplating for a while, 'Meet us here, by this seat, tomorrow evening at seven o'clock. Bring me a sailor's hat from the *Aurora*. It must have *Aurora* on –'

'That would be extremely difficult,' Konstantin interrupted. 'Impossible! We don't know anyone in the crew of the *Aurora*, and, even if we did, he wouldn't give us his hat.'

'Do it,' Tim said to Yuri, 'and I'll give you *two* sweaters.'

'What's up with you?' Colin asked, over vodkas in the hotel bar. Normally Tim was the most decent of people; fair, generous, lovable, and as a friend and travelling companion, the best. Why on earth should he want to persecute a penniless young Russian? The nights *were* still cold, as Yuri had said – it was late April – and, Colin noticed, the boy wasn't wearing a sweater under his jacket. Nor was Konstantin. Perhaps they didn't own a sweater between them.

The *Aurora*, the most famous of all Russian ships, had fired the first shot in the Revolution of 1917. It was nowadays moored in the River Neva and was one of Leningrad's biggest tourist attractions. Its crew – such as might exist to man it in its present function – would undoubtedly be ultra spit-and-polish; *not* likely to exchange an article of uniform for anything.

'Queen. Princess Aurora,' Colin said. He was trying to laugh Tim out of his mood. 'Princess Aurora Timofeyevna, tsaritsa of all the Russias.'

Tim did not even smile. 'Buy me another drink,' he said. 'Coll-doll.'

'We've got your hat,' Yuri announced. He looked very pleased with himself. He pulled it out of a paper bag – an imitation sailor's hat he had probably bought in a toyshop, and the name on it was not *Aurora*, but *Perm*.

'I'm sorry,' Tim said. 'It won't do. A bargain is a bargain; I asked for a *real* hat from the *real* Aurora.'

'We told you that was out of the question,' Konstantin said.

'I'm sorry,' Tim repeated. He stood up and walked off, in the direction of the park gates. Colin glanced at the Russians' unhappy faces, squeezed Konstantin's hand, then hurried after Tim.

'Why are you doing this?' he said. 'For all you know, he might have spent his last rouble on that hat! He's only a kid!'

'A bargain is a bargain.'

'Rubbish!'

'I get so tired of you. Every holiday we have together, you're chasing boys. It was the same in Prague. Seville. Florence. Geneva. And as for Munich. . .'

'You're quite at liberty to do it yourself.' He was puzzled: it wasn't the reason.

Tim stopped. 'Do you know what day it is?'

'Something . . . special?'

'The fifth anniversary of Martin's death.'

'Oh, Christ! Yes . . . I'd forgotten. I'm sorry.' Martin, Tim's lover for ten years, had died of AIDS.

Yuri and Konstantin caught up with them. 'We wanted to say we are still your friends,' Yuri said, holding out his hand.

Tim took off his jacket. Then his sweater. 'What now?' Colin asked.

'You can take off your sweater too,' Tim said. Colin obeyed, and Tim gave it to Konstantin. Then handed his own to Yuri. They were thick white Arans that had cost forty pounds each – they had bought them in Selfridges a month ago; they would need such things, they'd decided, in frozen Russia.

They talked for ten minutes with Yuri and Konstantin about nothing in particular – what they had seen and done in Leningrad; palaces, cathedrals, museums – then shook hands and parted. On their way to the hotel, now wearing only thin shirts under their jackets, they shivered a great deal.

'Don't ask me why I did that,' Tim said, gruffly. '*Never* ask me! End of story.'

Colin had just dozed off for the night when he was woken by a knock on the door. 'Come in,' he said, assuming it was Tim with an explanation of why he had changed his mind. 'How the hell did you get in here?' he gasped. It was Konstantin.

'Sssh!' Konstantin shut the door behind him, then tiptoed across the room. 'When Tim took off his jacket,' he whispered, 'his hotel pass fell out of the inside pocket. Here it is.' He sat down on the bed. 'You promised me some condoms. Do you think . . . I could use one now?'

Colin helped him undress, beginning with the sweater.

SACRAMENTO BLUES

I begin to forget what August and September are like in England; for four of the last five years these months have been spent on the edge of the Pacific Ocean. Only an eight-week trip this time, no work to do, no obligations – just visiting old friends and renewing my acquaintance with gay Mecca, ancient landscapes, smog and freeway concrete. Phil, my Vietnamese lover, is overjoyed to see me. Yet, already, after only four days, I'm homesick. I don't understand it. It never occurs when I travel in Europe; I lived for a year in the Jura Mountains in a tiny, remote village near the Swiss border, encapsulated in a wholly alien way of life and not once did I feel an urge to be back home. But I was a lot younger then. Homesickness, not wrinkling skin or declining sexual powers, is a cross of middle age.

Dennis and Paul, much to my regret, have sold their house on Twenty-first Street and moved to a characterless suburb of Sacramento. Instead of the incomparable view of San Francisco Bay and the coloured roof-tops of Castro village, they have Strip City – the same service stations, restaurants, banks, shopping malls in endless ribbons that line the endless highways that stretch across the whole three thousand miles of America. Give or take the difference in climate and vegetation, we could be in New Mexico, Maine, South Dakota, Wisconsin: anywhere. Britain's cities, of course, have features that

99

are utterly depressing. Twentieth-century Birmingham, Leeds, or Southampton are all fairly similar, and of less convenience to the consumer than any American equivalent: parking the car is a much bigger problem, and the restaurant chains and supermarkets are unspeakable. But they occupy a lot less space than here: here the land is squandered. And they aren't so exactly alike. Central Leeds isn't wholly the same as central Southampton, not nearly so much as Bakersfield, California and North Platte, Nebraska.

For Dennis and Paul the move made sense. Retired from work now, they are looking to the needs of old age. The garden is easier to manage and has a swimming pool; there are no stairs inside, no steep hills outside. And Sacramento, being less popular to live in than the Bay cities, has real estate prices that are not ridiculous. This house is bigger than their old one and has every modern luxury; yet it cost so little they bought it for cash with the profit they made on the Twenty-first Street sale. They like it here.

Phil and I are house-sitting while Dennis and Paul are visiting their families in Oregon. The heat in the Sacramento Valley in August is so punishing – one hundred and seven degrees today – that everything in tubs and pots on the deck, even the indoor plants, needs constant watering. That is all we are required to do. We can relax: swim in the pool, help ourselves to their liquor, explore tourist Sacramento (and there is some; it isn't all Strip City), pick up the threads of our relationship, make love.

But . . . maybe some of the reasons are purely physical, the shock to the system of being last week in London and now in the capital of California. Is it the vast distance from roots? Acclimatization takes longer than one imagines. Jet-lag means broken sleep that in turn breeds more broken sleep: I wake at four a.m. and stay tired all day. I never quite catch up. I drink more than I do at home; alcohol is so cheap. But California white wine wrecks my stomach; it's so acid I invariably get indigestion, and that also destroys my sleep. The sun soon tans my skin; I like the colour but I'm dry and itchy – as if I had a reptile's skin that has been too long out of water. The heat makes me want sex several times a day, and I haven't touched that beautiful Vietnamese body since Christmas: then tiredness spoils it. I am like a torpid bat. I need to go to a gym; only vigorous exercise will tune me up, put the mind at rest. But I can't face the ordeal of searching out a gym in a city I don't know, where I'll be for only a few days. I look at my watch more often than I need to, and see it's midnight in England now: are my friends still awake; has Ulrich got a man in his bed tonight? Not that I care, though I hope he's taking all the necessary precautions. There are no pinpricks of jealousy, no naggings of possessiveness – but he's probably enjoying it more than I am with Phil.

We spend the heat of the day doing the minimum – we water the plants, write letters, flop into the pool. Phil enjoys this – he is one of the world's slowest men, the person least suited to decisive action. I'm making mental comparisons between him and Ulrich as usual. For middle age is finding with increasing certainty that I don't need a live-in, till-death-do-us-part lover as Dennis has Paul, and Paul has Dennis. I don't value their dependence as much as I value my independence. Ulrich used to live with me, but after a while he found his own flat. Middle age is being fussy in my house, not wanting it disturbed by another man's clutter, not having to clear up the mess he makes in my kitchen.

Ulrich and Phil are not at all alike. Ulrich is a German of the blondest Aryan kind, and the most satisfactory part of our relationship is sex. Sex is its keystone, its raison d'être. His smooth boy's body is a marvel. One would think, after the two and a half years I've known him, that the physical would pall while other aspects would improve. It's the opposite. I like the sex more and more with the passing of time, but. . . many ingenious lovely things are gone. Trust. Respect. Not trust in his emotional fidelity to me; that never changes – but trust in his ability to tell the truth. The way he handles his life is not honest. His feelings for Germany are also those of the

101

blond Aryan: he admires Hitler, dislikes Jews. I find this incomprehensible. I detest it.

There are good points, of course. Drive, decisiveness, adaptability, a sweet temper, social ease. He doesn't irritate me in the minor details of life as Phil does. Phil fritters his existence away: as much as Ulrich tries to impose order and purpose on his. In traffic jams he's in the slow lane; he's always late for work; there is never enough time for living when the morning shower takes so long and the evening disappears in sorting out laundry. He's good with presents, but neglects to buy groceries. I arrive at an apartment where gifts have been chosen with care and are beautifully wrapped, but there's nothing to eat. He's constantly looking in mirrors, fiddling with his hair. Misses the exit he wants on the freeway because he's become too engrossed in a song on the radio. Should he change his job or not? Nobody in my life have I spent longer waiting around for. Is all this peculiarly Oriental? A reaction to the tragic years in Saigon, the escape, the near-death from thirst? Having reached America makes him feel he has arrived not at a beginning but a final summation, and nothing else matters very much? I don't know. He talks little about the last days in Vietnam: selling his body for food, dodging the bombs, fighting for a place on the boats. It haunts his nightmares, however. He wakes in a sweat, crying out, brains jammed: and calms, slowly, as the things of the room cease to be mortar fire, shell holes, corpses.

He has a delicious sense of humour, and is delicate in all those dealings with people where Ulrich is heavy-handed. He's the personification of kindness, gentleness and honesty. Incapable of being devious. Politically as left as Ulrich is of the right. I trust him absolutely.

Both are aware of the other's existence and place in my life. They speak of each other contemptuously; even the virtues I see they regard as faults. They have met: and they behaved with impeccable courtesy. Phil even went so far as to invite Ulrich to dinner; Ulrich very politely (he'd love to, but a prior engagement) refused. Both men have one thing in common: an overwhelming desire to make me abandon the other.

That they should want me to be so totally committed seems odd considering they are my juniors by almost two decades. But to search for permanence and stability, 'marriage,' is perfectly understandable in men in their twenties. I thought so too. And found it twice. Each lasted seven years, and against all odds we tried to make it work. After the second one finished, I had little desire for more of the same. Middle age is confidence to live alone, not to need someone as security, anchor, the meaning of life. Work is more important. My house, my privacy, my friends.

And sex. Yes, that, if I had no lover, could be the problem: it isn't that I can't go out and find a nice young thing for a night; I know that I probably can, but the spectre of AIDS. . . And the boring hunt I no longer want: that as a priority on Friday or Saturday instead of drinking, dancing, and conversation. Of course I could, by sheer accident, meet the perfect man, though the job specifications grow tougher as the years pass. He would have to have Ulrich's drive and decisiveness, Phil's sweetness and honesty; he would – if I wanted to love, respect, admire, understand, share – probably have to be a creative or a performing artist, a Baryshnikov or a Hockney (though much better-looking), someone involved in his own world of work, who rarely wanted my intrusion or I his. We would talk on the phone weekdays, but from Friday to Sunday and on vacations we'd shut out the rest of the world. We would not live together, but simply be guests in each other's houses. He would never be jealous, moody, dissembling, dithery. And it goes without saying that he would have a perfect body, with curly hair as blond as Ulrich's or be as olive-skinned, as almond-eyed as Phil. I've never met this man. Not in London or Paris or Berlin or Sydney or L.A. or New York or San Francisco, and even more certainly not in the pages of porn magazines. He doesn't exist.

'If you don't take the possible things, then you get nothing,' I once read in a novel.

I look over the fence at the parched grass of a derelict field. The Sacramento Valley is as flat as Holland, but it isn't Amsterdam I see on the horizon, just more of Strip City. Phil is in the pool, lying on an air-bed, naked, his eyes closed.

'Why don't we go out and do something?' I suggest.

'Sure.' And, to my surprise, he climbs out of the pool with movements that are almost energetic.

Something turns out to be Old Sacramento, a refurbished area of downtown that has been made to look as it was a hundred years ago. It's pleasant and pretty, though very tourist-orientated with too many cafés and gift shops. I buy a brass corkscrew because it's so weird, so vulgar – a naked youth: his head lifts the tops off bottles, his cock unscrews the corks (which means it's twice as long as his body.) The late afternoon sun is not oppressive: the sensation on my skin is now most agreeable. We visit the railroad museum. Well worth it: ancient American trains from the Virginia City/Truckee Railroad – wide wood-burning smokestacks, snowplough/cowcatcher in front. I've only seen such things in the books of my childhood, and here they are, real, and beautifully restored, new paint gleaming: black, red, gold. I feel once again, as I do looking at Victorian houses in San Francisco, a pleasure in nineteenth-century artefacts that I don't often experience in Britain – so much care and loving patience has been taken with the manufacture of each one that the result is not just a thing that functions; it is a work of art.

Phil discovers that he's locked his keys inside his car for the second time in two weeks. He's thrown completely off balance, is so cast down that he's incapable for a while of any sort of action. 'What shall I *do*?' he asks.

'Phone Triple A.' (The American Automobile Association.) 'Are you a member?'

'No.'

'Then you should be.' Irritation at his helplessness stunts my sympathy.

'I called Triple A last time,' he says. 'They charged twenty dollars! Now another twenty! I can't *afford* the waste of money!'

'I don't see what else you can do.'

He goes off to phone. I sit on a fire hydrant, basking in the heat. Exchange smiles with a man who's obviously looking for a pick-up. His legs are thin. Phil is away so long I cross the road to see what he is doing.

He's searching through the directory. 'I can't find the fucking number!' he wails. He is nearly in tears. I find it for him, and say to myself *I'm* the visitor; I shouldn't be the one to point out freeway exits, show him A.A.A. in the phone book. By now, Ulrich (if he ever locked his keys inside his car, which is doubtful) would have got Triple A out here on the job and be haggling over the price.

But Ulrich wouldn't have been able to laugh at himself as Phil does later when his good mood is restored, nor been such fun to dance with at the disco we find on Sacramento's K Street; his movements and my movements would not have made the pair Phil and I are on a dance floor.

Too tired tonight to make love. But I'm awake at four; bad dreams and the automatic sprinklers on the lawn have disturbed me. Phil is sound asleep. I get out of bed, and stare at my body in the bathroom's full-length mirror. It will do. The muscles – particularly the biceps and the tits – are firm enough. The stomach will never be a flat, clear, downward line again, but a waist measurement of thirty-one at my age isn't a recipe for despair. There are many furrows around the neck, but I like them. The face has high cheek-bones and more furrows, deep ones: they tell me I've lived. The cock: has served me well enough, though it doesn't always like my alcohol consumption. Sometimes cancels out the brain's messages, and obstinately refuses to exert itself. It isn't small. It isn't big. I have to confess if a cock is minute or unappealing I don't want to help it to orgasm, let alone think of it as belonging to a potential lover. Why do people try to make one feel guilty about this? An attractive cock, though it isn't the

105

major criterion, is one of the reasons why one wants to have sex with a man.

I'm comfortable inside this old torso. It will do for another decade or three. What am I trying to figure out? That if I lose both my lovers, I'll still be a fair proposition, a marketable commodity? I can talk someone into it – can't I? Anyway, I sometimes pass for 'young' in a flattering light, though why age is with many men an obsessively important criterion, I don't understand. I recently overheard in a bar a conversation between two pretty young things neither of whom I'd have kicked out of bed: 'I couldn't *possibly* go with a man who's older than twenty-four!' said one; 'Yes, that's far too old,' the other agreed. Stupid fools! They don't realise what they could be missing: expertise, experience. But I was like that too, I remember.

How do Ulrich and Phil view it? Not, evidently, as so many men of their age – that a lover should be of the same years as they are, that that is the only method of ensuring mutual interests and attitudes, is the only good way to pass the time between now and death. In choosing a foreigner and a man so much their senior they have – perhaps subconsciously – put an escape clause into things, though Ulrich may have thought about it and with typical over-confidence said to himself, 'Oh, I can handle that!' Phil, totally uncalculating, would simply show surprise that such matters should be considered. As for me, I've never had a lover the same age as me. Every one has been younger. I'm just as guilty, therefore, of ageism as the two pretty things I listened to in the bar.

I wander into the kitchen and make tea, smoke a cigarette. Why is even the cheapest, most ordinary tea-bag from Sainsbury or Tesco superior to any you buy in America? American tea is dry, dusty, tasteless. The penalty, perhaps, for throwing all those chests of it into the harbour at Boston.

Phil appears, yawning. 'What are you doing?' he asks.

'Drinking tea.'

'Why?'

'Why not?'

'Come back to bed and screw me.'

It's really good. I gasp, fall back, and a moment later, for the first time since leaving England, I'm profoundly, dreamlessly asleep.

It's nine thirty before we get out of bed, and the morning trickles away – we forage for breakfast, shave, shower, water the plants, lie on the air-bed in the pool. Phil reads a novel. He has to have glasses now for reading: they suit him.

At noon Dennis and Paul arrive quite unexpectedly – they are a day early. 'We cut it short,' Paul says. 'We wanted to see you!'

A year since we met. The conversation is excited, all of us talking together: the stories, the jokes, stored up for months to release now. Hugs and kisses. 'God, I need a drink!' Dennis decides, and we start on the vodka. Suddenly the afternoon is half gone.

'And we haven't even unpacked!' Paul exclaims. Then begins a long story about the relatives he has been visiting. He has four sisters in Portland, Oregon, all married, and so many nephews and nieces, most of them also married, it's difficult to keep count.

I persuade Phil, who's reluctant, to leave them for a while so they can sort out their luggage, the mail, the phone messages. He is sprawled by the pool, a Stetson rakishly on his head, his eyes glazed. A silly grin. I know the signs: too much booze. But it's our last chance to visit the Capitol; it would be absurd to leave Sacramento without looking at California's seat of government. I promise to cook dinner when we return.

It's impressive, particularly the decor of its interior, though I do wonder why nearly all the parliaments of the Union resemble St Paul's cathedral – is a dome absolutely necessary to give the right touch of solemnity, the illusion of monumental grandeur? We inspect the Governors' portraits. Ronald Reagan looks as if he is striving a little too hard for that genial, avuncular pose he later came to wear as easily as his skin; and I'm amused that he's virtually hidden under a staircase. Perhaps the Democrat administration of California doesn't want to be reminded.

I look at my watch. One a.m. in England: Ulrich asleep, and I hope not alone.

More drinks with Dennis and Paul. Alcohol destroys timing, and the result is burned dinner. The pork is charcoal, the French fries black, the squash so squashed it melts in the mouth more quickly than ice cream. 'It's delicious!' Paul says. Without irony, as far as I can tell.

'Excellent,' Dennis assures me as he chews rock-hard meat. If they are being honest they're even more drunk than I am.

Phil, however, keeps up a battery of rude comments and jokes throughout the whole meal. 'It's awful!' he says. '*Aw*-ful!'

Sleeping, and waking next day, I'm still homesick. After alcohol is invariably a depressant. Sunday morning, and we're all very quiet. Breakfast is boiled eggs and toast cooked by Dennis, and other bland, wholesome foods that won't hurt tender stomachs. Another day drifts on, is lost. Why do I always have this need to do something with time, to say at nightfall I've achieved this or that? Such a concept never enters Phil's head. It's one a.m. in England again, and Ulrich will have set his alarm for seven: tomorrow is a work day.

We say our farewells to Dennis and Paul, then leave.

After Sacramento my spirits begin to lift. Maybe it was the days of inaction at Anystreet, Strip City that triggered the blues; the flat, dull plain: the excessive heat. Driving to the South Bay we stop at the Concord Pavilion – a big, open-air arena which reminds me a little of the Hollywood Bowl – and listen to Laura Branigan. I don't think she will become a Diana Ross, a Donna Summer – her act does not convince; she has no charisma, just great difficulty in keeping her hair in place: she fusses with it more frequently than Phil with his. But I like the voice and the songs, and I'm amazed at the power of her lungs; she's a second Ethel Merman. Sitting here in shorts and tee-shirt in the warm darkness, a full moon overhead pale as bone, I feel for the first time this trip that I'm in touch with my sort of West Coast: experiences I'd never have in London.

We are house-sitting again, in Aptos, near Santa Cruz. Five minutes' walk from New Brighton Beach; the mornings are cool and overcast: the lawns are green and when I turn on the sprinklers I have the illusion of rain on the windows and England. By the house telephone is a cryptic message: 'Al Swensen has taken back his weed-eater.' A cousin of the ant-eater? Why do we not have such a useful animal in Stoke Newington?

On the beach, alone, early morning. Grey sea, grey sky; moored yachts in distant Santa Cruz are grey etchings. Fog. Away to the left is an old hulk which is now the home of scores of pelicans. I can pick up fossils by the thousand under the cliffs here; shells of the utmost delicacy embedded in stone. If I am caught removing them I can be thrown in jail, but that does not deter me. Huge tangles of sea-weed show the high tide mark. Zillions of anchovies all week have been hurling themselves like lemmings at the shore, and today is no exception: seals' heads bob up everywhere, and birds in a frenzy of excitement hover, squawk, flap, plunge and feast. Terns, their beaks miniature scissors, drop into the sea like kamikaze pilots. Sea-ducks, gulls. Pelicans, majestic and delicate as gigantic petals, float on air currents, defying gravity it seems, then swoop, trawl up hundreds of fish. They often fly in threes or sevens, follow-my-leader. ('Because,' Phil, absurdly, says, 'their sexual appetites are *voracious*!') Where they choose to stab the sea's patina, other birds follow in frantic swarms: acknowledging that pelicans know best.

I have to let these two lovers, in their own good time, leave me. They deserve a better man than me, one who can offer them what they need. Middle age is letting go without rancour, without selfishly saying, 'What am I losing? I may not find anything else.' It's knowing it is good to be alone and anchorless, that no experience is a waste of time, that 'too late' is not a viable concept.

The pelicans swoop at the right moments, and in between they lazily drift. As they slice the water, their wings fold as the pages of a book close. Pelicans are wisdom. A long way off, two thousand miles off, in the direction I'm looking, is Hawaii.

So much to enjoy. So much.

THE ROAD TO HANA

For Tom Holt

Will I discover that the Earth is flat after all? Drop off the edge into tomorrow?

First impressions are not favourable. We are two and a half thousand miles west of the American continent – three time zones and five hours' flying from San Francisco. I had expected something different therefore, but Honolulu and Waikiki, now so built up that the one runs into the other, are much like any American city. Less litter, perhaps, and really fresh air, but there are freeways, traffic jams, tower blocks, Woolworths, Macdonalds, Pizza Hut, Burger King, Kentucky Fried Chicken, Pay'n Save, Arco, Chevron, etcetera, etcetera. A line from *The Cherry Orchard* comes into my head; it is Trofimov, the penniless eternal student informing Lopahin, the rich builder who wants to cut down the trees and erect holiday homes, that he is necessary only as a monster that devours everything in its path is necessary.

At the hotel desk the first difference. The clerk is a native Hawaiian and has none of the warmth, friendliness and welcome one has come to regard as normal from almost anybody one meets on the mainland. He is polite: icily polite. During the next few days we find that this is the most we can expect. Native Hawaiians, apart from those we meet in gay situations, are not fond of tourists, even though they have to earn their living from visitors.

111

They are on the whole unhelpful, inefficient, and at times downright rude. It's understandable. They were in the middle of the path being trodden by the monster that devours everything. They resisted. They killed Captain Cook and sacrificed three of Vancouver's men to the gods, but it didn't help. Exploited in the last century by New England missionaries and their sons, the big businessmen who never went home, Hawaii was annexed by a United States that had forgotten its anti-colonial origins and saw only the best site for a naval base in the entire Pacific Ocean. With their land now turned into sugar plantations and pineapple fields, the Hawaiians refused to work for the foreign invader; they grew sick, died, dwindled in number, and today form only a fifth of the population. We are told that Hawaii is proud to be the fiftieth state of the Union. American Hawaii is doubtless proud, but that other fifth seems to live in smouldering resentment.

Janos and Jim find their room has twin beds, and they had asked for a double. 'You go down to that hotel desk right now,' Janos says, 'and tell them we *demand* a double!'

'Why me?' Jim asks. 'Why not you?'

Janos grins. 'You're supposed to be the man about the house!'

'Oh . . . O.K.' Jim will do anything for a quiet life. He is successful – I'm astonished, for this is not a gay hotel – and fifteen minutes later the two of them are moving their stuff into the room next door. I go to my single room and consult Bob Damron, the indispensable guide to gay America. Yes, we are only one block from a popular bar and a good disco. I want to touch Polynesian skin. But Janos and Jim have other purposes; they are seriously thinking of uprooting themselves from their adopted San Francisco and settling here. Though we are at the moment on Oahu, Honolulu Airport being virtually the only arrival point, we are to fly in three days' time to the island of Maui, where Janos and Jim want to look at property for sale. All I know about Maui is that it has a vast number of pineapple fields and a huge, dormant volcano.

Outside Waikiki and Honolulu the monster has left the coast undevoured: I have never, anywhere else in the world, seen such beautiful beaches, such superb sea. The water is like the Aegean, blue-black, at times almost totally black, but near the shore, as the waves race over sand and coral reef, there are the most subtle gradations of turquoise and thirsty pale blue. The air temperature is ninety, the sea a tepid bath. On almost every beach it is possible to surf. The choppy restlessness of the water is the result of the constant wind – completely satisfying to the ear and the eye. White scribbles on the sea, perpetually changing, making new patterns, shapes: I'm reminded of the shell fossils imprisoned in stones at New Brighton – inscrutable alphabets, urgent incomprehensible messages. I hire a board, but fear my skill may be rusty; it's years since I did this, though once I was a surf freak – I couldn't get enough of it. But, as with riding a bicycle, the techniques are never lost, the knack, the sense of timing. I am in and out of the sea all day, surfing till I'm exhausted. Lying on the sand afterwards is not unlike the sensation when a long boat trip finishes; the ground seems to be moving – I feel drenched, walls of water pouring over me, though I am dry, lying on a towel absorbing sun.

Our favourite beach is below the lighthouse on Diamond Head, which, we are told, is gay and nude. It's neither, but that doesn't matter. Just the three of us, the young Tahitian, Félix, I met last night, and a dozen others: sand, sea, wind, surf.

Paradise.

But any true paradise has to contain a serpent. On Oahu there are several serpents. The dreary squares of sugar cane and pineapple: the white man's industries. Pineapple is a dull fruit, its juice sweet enough, but its texture is coarse and unpleasant. Fields of it are like fields of grey iron spikes – mines. The debasing of the ancient Hawaiian art of wood carving: tatty little statues in the shops of bare-breasted grinning grass-skirt girls to decorate Mid-West mantelpieces. Postcards and

113

calendars of more bare-breasted girls, and – presumably for the gay tourist – naked Hawaiian men, coquettish, legs akimbo so the cock is invisible: silly. Shopping malls, identikit versions of those in California, out of the same shopping-mall factory I guess, with the same stores – pleasant enough these redwood structures with their central courtyards, trees and flowers, where you can buy a coca cola, a coffee; but what are they doing *here*? We eat the same kind of pizza we could eat in several places in San Francisco: towards the end of the meal I notice a rat running along the woodwork, and I tell the waiter what I have seen.

He shrugs his shoulders. 'We have them all the time,' he says. 'You can't get rid of them on Oahu.' (He is a white American, and his tone of voice as he says "Oahu" is one of superiority.) 'It's a ground-floor business, this restaurant. They come in through the front door.'

Strangest excuse for the presence of rats I've ever heard. *Come in through the front door?* This one popped out of the ceiling.

Janos and Jim have a serpent. Apart from quarrels (not serious) and endless analysing of their relationship, they have arranged to meet one of Janos's multitudinous brothers on Maui; Laszlo and his wife, Beth, are there on a fortnight's holiday. Janos came out to his family a year ago, and, although the initial reaction was not horror and disgust, they have been less than supportive. Dad said Janos was welcome home at any time, but *not* to bring any of his friends; Mom just talks as if his gayness doesn't exist, while the siblings don't bother, apart from Christmas and his birthday, to keep in touch at all. Janos is apprehensive about the meeting, and wants Jim and me to be with him. Jim is curious (so am I), but coming from different backgrounds – we both found it easier to come to terms with our families' neglect of us when they discovered our homosexuality – it's difficult to understand why it's so important to Janos, who has, during the past year, been alternately angry and sad at the reception his announcement produced.

114

'What else did you think?' Jim says. 'It's all very usual. Alas – but it *is*.' I agree.

AIDS is our worst serpent. The Tahitian and I therefore play it very safe, but it is so good, and he is so nice, so beautiful, that I am almost ready to abandon England and do a Gauguin; disappear with him for ever to some South Sea island. I hire a car and tour Oahu with him, stopping at any good beach we find for a quick swim and a few moments' surfing. He is a delight to watch as he toys with the waves, teasing them, rejecting one for its bigger follower; he is born, it would seem, to walk on water.

It is a day of sea and sky, of dramatic green mountains, groves of bananas, banyan trees, papaya, coconuts, flowers – hibiscus, bougainvillaea, orchids, morning glory, ginger, hundreds of species I can't identify – their colours soft salmon pink, blushing red, orange, deepest purple, gold, ice blue, wedding-dress white: dazzling, exotic, delicate. Delicate: that is a word that applies to everything native here. Even the men are boyish, fragile. How long will the monster let them last?

The monster didn't have his own way all the time. Pearl Harbor, December the seventh, 1941. ('The day the Second World War started,' says our tour guide. Has he not heard of Hitler, Poland, the fall of France? Janos and Jim condemn the chauvinism – 'You get it all the time,' says Jim; 'We Americans are so isolationist, so inward-looking,' says Janos – then they laugh at *my* irritated British chauvinism.) Was 1941 perhaps the ultimate penalty for stealing the place from the Hawaiians? We are on a boat, cruising round the harbour, which, in fact, is an inlet of the sea that loops deep into Oahu. It opens out into a wide lake which has an island in its centre, bristling with military installations. It's characteristic of American openness that we are allowed to observe all this and photograph it – I cannot imagine such a possibility at Chatham or Devonport. Over the loudspeakers of our boat a commentary on the events of 1941 is relayed; it is detailed, accurate, and fair to the Japanese skill in planning and executing the infamous attack. On board, however, are groups of Japanese tourists who, as time passes, look increasingly ill at ease and glum. The destroyed battleships are still on the muddy bottom, though not much, except for the *Nevada*, is visible. The memorial to the dead straddles the *Arizona* in which more than a thousand sailors lie entombed. One of them is my mother's cousin, Thade Coakley. We stop; the last post sounds through the loudspeakers, and the captain throws the traditional Hawaiian tribute onto the water – a lei, a wreath of flowers. It's a moving few minutes, and I recall how differently I felt on arriving at Honolulu Airport: a lei was placed around my neck, and I was photographed with a scantily clad Polynesian girl, lei round *her* neck, flowers in her hair. 'You wouldn't have grumbled,' Janos said, 'if it had been a Polynesian boy.' He's wrong: the degrading of what was once a custom of significance, the traditional welcome, into a bit of commercialized trivia for tourists would have made me feel embarrassed whoever it was at my side.

My mind is still full of serpent/paradise images, so I'm amused to read that there are no snakes on Hawaii. Obvious, if one thinks about it: in the beginning birds flew to these islands, insects in their feathers, and animals would have been brought by early Polynesian man. But snakes, unless the Stone-agers were crazy enough to bring them on their rafts, would not, like other life forms, have had transport for the voyage. At Hanauma Bay my lover and I don snorkelling equipment. The sea is full of tame fish – shoals of little rainbow-coloured creatures, of larger white flat fish like cod, of long wriggling eel-like things, all inquisitive, unafraid, friendly: another illusion of time was, of pre-serpent paradise, of man and all beasts living in harmony. Under the water my Tahitian and I embrace, put our arms round each other, lie body against body, and the sweet solemn-faced fish stare, flick their tails, slide over and under us, rub mouths on our skins.

116

There is a lack of American efficiency. Signposts are confusing or do not exist; buses don't always go to the destinations indicated; and people you ask for directions are very hazy about distance and time. We ask a man we meet at the lighthouse how far it is to the nearest store. 'A quarter of a mile down the road,' he says. It turns out to be over two miles away. Worried that the bus which is meant to terminate at Honolulu Airport is shuttling us off to somewhere else, Janos asks the driver if the airport is the last stop.

'No,' is the abrupt reply.

'The next to last stop?'

'No.'

'Are you going to the airport?'

The driver does not answer. We get there eventually, but it takes twice as long as we have been told, and the route is roundabout, almost haphazard. We arrive for our flight to Maui with only ten minutes to spare.

The plane is full of beautiful people, and I am reminded again of the Aegean Sea, of the boats returning at nightfall to Mykonos, their decks crowded with the world's polyglot, hedonistic young – the suntanned limbs, the unlined faces. Here they are once more with their rucksacks, sandals, innocent eyes and golden skin. Their hair is not so long as it was a decade ago. In couples: there are no family groups on this plane. The flight is a mere half hour, but the steward serves us all with chilled white wine and Hawaiian punch, free of charge.

The monster has not yet eaten Maui although he has made a start – an airport at Kahului, a few good roads, hotels, motels, Kentucky Fried Chicken, Woolworths, shopping malls – but Lahaina still has the atmosphere of the whaling town it once was, with laid-back characters, ancient wooden buildings, and an old clipper moored in the harbour. There are no freeways, high-rise flats, nuclear installations or traffic jams – yet. A banyan tree of vast dimensions is the town centre. In a waterfront shop I buy a tiger shark's jaws for six dollars, and give it to Félix, who is delighted. There is even a gay bar. Lahaina, I imagine, has always been tolerant of the off-beat; pineapple growers and missionaries were less important to its prosperity than sailors. I'm much more at home here than in Waikiki or Honolulu.

We go to the Organ Grinder, a restaurant with tables on a verandah overlooking the sea. An elderly Korean woman, so emaciated she could have just been released from work on the Burma railway, comes up to our table and asks, 'Are you boys here to eat or to drink?'

'A bit of both, I guess,' Jim says. 'Why?'

'Because I have to do the goddam cooking, that's why!' She roars with laughter, showing gums without teeth.

We order scallops and wine, and wonder what on earth the meal will be like. She doesn't exactly look clean, and spends almost no time in the kitchen: on every occasion we glance up she's drinking and smoking with diners at other tables. But when the food appears, it is excellent.

Afterwards we drive round the bay to Kihea; the sunset will be more dramatic across the water than at Lahaina. Huge dark clouds are sweeping in obliterating Maui's two summits – the giant volcano, Haleakala, and Iao, the smaller peak that dominates the western edge of the island and which looks remarkably like Skiddaw. We stop by a windswept beach, and think we've chosen the wrong place, the only bit of coast in Hawaii so far that is uninviting. There is more stone than sand, uncomfortable, sharp volcanic stone that makes walking difficult; and there is an unpleasantly pungent smell of sea-weed – iodine, presumably, but the resemblance is to sewage. However, unpropitious beginnings here invariably lead to something worthwhile: the stone peters out and we are treading on sand; the smell vanishes. The beach becomes fringed with wind-blown palms. The sea is rough, ideal for surfing, the evening sun giving it the appearance of beaten pewter or lead, a dull gold constantly flickering on a surface of metal. The horizon is colours that change minute by minute, crimson, orange, pink; the hurtling cloud that obscures Iao is black, grey, pelican brown against a cold greenish sky. Ahead of us two young men stride into

118

the sea with surfboards and sails, and shoot across the water towards the sunset. Their boards jump clean out of the waves and they still cling on, almost horizontally; they spin the sails round one hundred and eighty degrees with a casual arrogance, a flick of the wrist, then scud back over the water so gracefully, so seemingly without effort, that we stop and stare with envious astonishment. Tomorrow I'm going windsurfing too, I say to myself.

Suddenly, without any warning at all, it begins to pour with rain. A brief, intense shower.

I do go windsurfing next day, albeit less expertly than those two guys, while Janos and Jim look at houses. With Félix and a man we met that evening in Lahaina's gay bar, a suntanned thirty-year-old blond, a Mormon drop-out. Not from Salt Lake City but Oahu, where Mormons colonised and converted almost as long ago as the New England Protestants; indeed founded and still run the Polynesian Cultural Centre, a museum of the crafts and cultures of many Pacific islands. Bill's parents work at the Centre, and he grew up in the village nearby. 'You cannot be Mormon and gay,' he says. So he took off for Lahaina, where he makes and sells sandals, surfs, drinks, has a lover, and feels generally comfortable. His parents never write or phone. 'I've ceased to care,' he says. 'They're more interested in money than people. Mormonism is about money. Big business. Did you know it costs fourteen dollars to go into the Centre?' Yes, I did, which is why I haven't been there. 'It's a zoo, really. Not genuine Polynesia, but the Pacific Stone Age kept alive in hermetically sealed conditions.'

'Was it hard, coming to terms?' I ask.

'Gay and Mormon? Sure.' He smiles. Dazzling white teeth. 'But I knew from the beginning which I had to be. Which I could do best. Not that that helps to heal the wounds.'

But the wounds have healed now, I think. And as a windsurfing companion he is also pretty good.

We drive to the top of Haleakala, the whole ten thousand and twenty-three feet of it, then stand on the rim and

119

gaze into the crater. We cannot see much; it is filled with rushing mist that looks alarmingly like smoke. Black ash everywhere – a dreamscape of shattered, twisted rocks. Because of the rarefied air, we experience a little breathlessness. People's cars only start with difficulty. Glimpses through the cloud of mysterious, distant islands – Hawaii, Molokai, Lanai, Kahoolawe. It is all a disappointment; from Lahaina early this morning the volcano was totally free of cloud, floating almost, like Mount Fuji: we had thought we'd see the whole archipelago and a hundred miles, in any direction, of the Pacific Ocean. Nothing.

During the descent it rains again, torrents of it, and despite the sugar and pineapples I'm reminded of England – wet green hill-slopes, grey fog, wind, Skiddaw/Iao.

So what is the big problem Janos has with his brother Laszlo and sister-in-law Beth? We spend a relaxed, warm, pleasant evening with them; notwithstanding the Hungarian Catholic origins, the provincial Montana upbringing in a conservative one-horse town where they still live, they are perfectly at ease in the company of four gay men. Neither has knowingly met a gay person before. We don't discuss sexual orientation, or the impact of Janos's coming out on his family, and there really isn't any need to do so; Laz and Beth simply accept Janos and Jim as a couple, me and Félix as a couple. What they may have said beforehand or afterwards I don't know, but I doubt it was belittling, condescending.

Janos thoroughly enjoys himself, and Jim looks pleased for hours.

'They're sure to report to Mom and Dad,' Janos says, as we stroll back to our hotel. 'It will be favourable!'

'It really doesn't matter one way or the other,' Jim says for the hundredth time.

The family resemblance is strong: I'm amused to think that if strangers were asked to guess which is the gay brother stereotypical reactions would make them pick out Laszlo. Something a mite less male about him – he doesn't have Janos's firm runner's legs nor his fit, well-honed chest and arms; his voice is not so deep; his face is more delicate, his personality shyer, more introvert. Yet this man at twenty was so sure of himself that he got married and ten years later is still happily married to the same woman; they have three sons, at present with Mom and Dad in Montana. So much for the idiocy of stereotyping.

'It's easier for straights of their age to accept,' Janos says. 'The real problem lies with the fifty-year-olds and up, the pensioners.'

Jim disagrees. 'I've never heard of a pensioner being involved in, for instance, gay-bashing.'

'Laz and Beth are humane, decent people,' I say. 'And that's all there is to it.'

'We have exactly the same problems in Tahiti,' Félix says.

The road to Hana is narrow, winding, mountainous and in a very bad state of repair: it takes two and a half hours to travel fifty miles. It would be quite possible to build a new road that would more than halve the time and soothe the nerves, but Hana people don't want that; the macadam is deliberately left to disintegrate in order to discourage the tourists, the real estate developers and the businessmen: to keep the monster out. I had imagined Hana lacked electricity, stores, restaurants, anything twentieth century, but it does not. There is a tiny airstrip not open to commercial traffic, and that is how it survives. The road journey is spectacular: rain forests, bamboo thickets, waterfalls, precipices; exotic birds, flowers and flowering shrubs in immense profusion and of every colour imaginable; and the wine-dark sea far below us with its scribbles of white like forgotten words.

The sand at Hana is black. Félix and I drive to the next beach where it is yellow, then sunbathe and surf the whole afternoon while Janos and Jim look at a house. When we rejoin them they are all smiles. 'We're going to take it,' Jim says.

Though Hana is the nearest thing to paradise that anyone is ever likely to see, I could not make communication with the rest of the world so difficult for myself. 'Are you sure?' I ask.

121

They nod. 'Why not come into the deal with us?' Janos says.

But I am London-bound, to Woolworths, Macdonalds, Kentucky Fried Chicken, tower blocks, traffic jams. 'It's tempting,' I say. 'Very tempting. Yes . . . keep the spare room empty. Meanwhile. . .'

As we depart on the fragile light plane, hopping from Maui to Oahu, I feel hope. The beauty of these islands hangs by a thread, but this thread the monster will find tough in his jaws. People like Janos and Jim, like Bill, like the inhabitants of Hana who refuse to build a good road, won't let the monster eat everything. Somewhere here there will always be rain forests, and hibiscus that is not just cultivated in botanical gardens; there will always be surf and surfers, wind rushing in palm leaves, cloud as I see it now from this tiny aeroplane's window on Molokai, Laina, Kahoolawe: daft Korean cooks, drop-outs, people like Félix. . .

I'll come back.

FLUX 1981

ONE

Not jee-vanch-ie but give-enchy; that was Andy's pro-
nunciation. Pierre Cardin became Perry Carding, whereas
Zendique and Lagerfeld were said correctly. It amused
me. There is still a slight trace of Givenchy in my
wardrobe; it's all that's left of him here.

I used to call him my bathroom queen. The hours we
spent sniffing after-shaves in Galeries Lafayette!

It's difficult to recall the first time I saw him. I think
it was the gay pub in Exeter, the Hope and Anchor,
on a crowded Saturday evening: wall-to-wall gays. Last
January, I think. He was talking to Martin and Graham,
old friends of mine, though not close friends, and he was
with a man who turned out to be his lover, Don. Martin
brought me into the conversation, but I don't remember
what was said. I do remember deciding that Andy and
Don were both mildly attractive, and asking myself which
I preferred. I forget if I answered my own question.

Mildly attractive? Extraordinary how obtuse I must have
been; Andy is undoubtedly one of the most beautiful guys
I have ever met, and I know that my opinion is not just
some weird quirk of personal taste. Going out with him,
to a pub or a disco that neither of us had visited before,
was a bizarre experience. He doesn't, yet, know the effect
he has, or how to deal with it – that's part of his charm.
Moths to a flame. I was always turning round to find a
stranger touching him, or dragging him onto the dance

123

floor; and, when he returned, he'd say, 'Where did *that* one come from?' or 'How can I get rid of *him*?' And then there was Neil, whom we met briefly in the William the Fourth in Hampstead, who spent a whole evening three days later, waiting for our plane from Paris to land at Heathrow. *Our* plane? He was waiting for Andy.

He's small, only five feet five, and he has long curly hair (looking after it keeps him for hours in the bathroom); very prominent high cheek-bones, and a slow lazy smile. Lovely peach-coloured skin. A distinctive walk, almost a lope, the result of a serious accident in mad eighteen-year-old biking days: a leg smashed in three places, months in hospital. When he's tired, the lope becomes a limp. His chief asset is his blue eyes. They say everything, far more than his mouth – for he rarely wastes words – and it irritates him that they reveal so much, telling the world at times what he'd rather conceal. I always knew without asking when he was interested, amused, weary, bored, satisfied, worried, happy: all the emotions. Except that of loving. At orgasm, yes. But loving: no.

We often talked about his eyes. 'What about mine?' I asked on one occasion.

'Yours?' He studied them for a moment. 'Also blue.'

'I know that!'

'They're mysterious.' He paused, then added, 'You're a mysterious person.'

'Am I? I think I'm transparent. Too much so for my own good.'

'No. You *do* have mystery, Paul. And I like that.'

He's twenty-one, twelve years my junior. A baker. And I'm an intellectual, a teacher. What on earth meeting-ground would we discover? We certainly found one, and the mental differences were not of the slightest importance. Something other than that broke it up.

I saw him again, a few weeks after we first met, at the club in Torquay. My old stomping-ground! So many memories. Chris. In February I was still in love with Chris. Unhappy, confused, deserted, looking for Mr. Right or at least Mr. Compromise and only finding Mr. Bed and Breakfast.

Torquay still bothered me: on the juke-box there – yes, a juke-box would you believe; the club's too small for a proper disco – they still played Chris-and-Paul's songs.

But that evening was pleasant enough, chatting and drinking with Andy and his lover, and Mark and Steve, and a boy called Bob who had arrived with Andy and Don. It was Bob's first venture ever into the gay world; and Mark wanted him. He didn't succeed. Bob I took for seventeen, eighteen at most, and when he asked me to dance and kissed me so passionately that I got really turned on, I was extremely surprised at his nerve. He was twenty-two he told me later.

Andy's beauty didn't register on that occasion, either. I lost little sleep on his account. I didn't see much of him in subsequent weeks – in the pub from time to time when, looking up from a drink or away from a dull conversation, I'd catch his eye and he'd smile. Mysteriously.

At a disco in March I was dancing with Roy. I love dancing with Roy; he is the only one of the whole Exeter crowd who really lets himself go on the floor, the only one with any stamina. Everybody else says, after a couple of records, 'I'm worn out; let's have a drink.' Roy and I peeled off our shirts; sweat poured; our jeans were glued to our legs. I noticed Andy staring at me.

That's him, I said to myself; that's the one I want. He's been here for weeks and I didn't realise.

We danced together that night, for the first time; then he returned to Don. He was wearing black leather trousers, and I remember thinking he must be dreadfully hot and sticky dancing in clothes like that. It was crazy to fall for Andy. He already had a lover, and though, as I watched from a distance, that particular affair seemed, if not exactly breaking apart, to be in a kind of doldrums, there was no evidence to suggest he was interested in me, except as another acquaintance on the local gay-go-round. I had no subtle plans, not even many daydreams, and a week would go by without thinking about him at all. March, in any case, was a good month; I was on holiday in the last week and went to Ireland with my Danish friend, Rolf. Rolf and I . . . that might possibly have come to something if Andy had not existed. Rolf, experienced, gentle, sweet: and he fell in love with me. Then *loved* me. But . . . but, but. Too gentle, perhaps? No magic. And sex just wasn't good enough. The relationship with Rolf turned out to be a mirror image of the relationship between me and Andy. Unfortunately for me, in the latter, I was playing Rolf.

Andy's greatest friend on the Exeter scene is Roger. I've known Roger for years, and though I don't see a lot of him, I always enjoy his company and wish we met more frequently. He's witty, intelligent – and a great gossip. He always knows the latest about who is sleeping with whom, sometimes, I think, even before the people concerned know it themselves. Not a person you tell much, therefore, but worth listening to. I met him one evening in the pub, and decided that this occasion would for once prove useful if I did let him know something.

'I'm after Andy Mackay,' I said. 'I don't want a one-night stand, a hole-in-the-corner quickie behind Don's back. I want an affair with him.'

I can't remember what Roger said, but all sorts of surprised expressions flitted across his face. The next time I saw Andy in the Hope and Anchor the eyes told me everything: I know, they said. I drank more than usual, and towards the end when people were leaving, I put my arms round him and said, 'Roger talked.'

'Yes. Shame I'm married.'

'I'd pinch you from Don if I could.'

'There's food for thought.' He walked away. Then returned. 'Be patient,' he said. 'Things aren't going so well between me and Don.'

Yes, that affair was now cracking up. They had been lovers for eight months, but they had never lived together. Don lived and worked in Plymouth, Andy in Exeter; there were forty miles of dual carriageway between them. They saw each other from Friday till Sunday, and occasionally during the week. They had gone on separate holidays at Christmas – Don had wanted that – he to the Canaries, Andy to Bournemouth. It was Andy who was trying to keep the relationship going, but it was a thankless task.

126

Friday was unusually quiet in the Hope. I was talking to some friends when Andy arrived with Roger. They stood against the wall, drinks in their hands, chattering, I was sure, about me. The eyes never left my face.

Roger left. 'Excuse me,' I said, interrupting Peter's monologue.

'I was scared you'd come over,' Andy said, laughing nervously.

'Scared?'

'Let's go in the other room. Then we can talk.'

So! I suddenly felt nervous too. Tense in the stomach. Not wanting to finish my beer.

A curious conversation, wary and probing on both sides. About relationships, in a vague, generalised way. 'What star sign are you?' he asked.

'Taurus.'

He laughed, and said, 'I don't think we'd be compatible.'

'Why not?'

'I'm Aries. April the third.'

'Do you take that sort of thing seriously?'

'No.'

'I'm glad to hear it.'

Then jewellery, clothes, after-shaves, perfumes: subjects we were later to return to, endlessly. Andy liked gold, diamonds; all Ariens did, he said.

'You'd cost me too much,' I told him.

'I wouldn't expect diamonds.' He looked at me, the eyes superbly mischievous. 'Yet.'

I drove him back to his flat. Outside, in the car, we kissed. Properly. For a long time. I had an erection three miles high.

'I must go,' he said. 'I have to work in the morning.'

'You can't send me home *now*!'

'I must. I have to be up at half past six.'

We kissed again. Tenderness. Desire. As much on his side as mine.

'If I don't leave now I'm done for,' he said.

'But . . . what does it matter?'

'It's nearly midnight.'

I should have insisted. Because, when we finally did get to bed, it was too planned, too calculated; that moment, then, was the right moment to start. If we had done so it might all, perhaps, have been just a little different.

'You must come over and see my house,' I said. 'It's beautiful. Cob and thatch. Two hundred years old.'

'I will.'

'Would you like to meet one night during the week?'

Wednesday, we decided. For a quiet drink somewhere.

TWO

Next morning I phoned Roger. I did not tell him much about the previous night; but I wanted information. Which, of course, he was more than ready to supply. Andy, he was fairly certain, wasn't interested. He liked me, yes, but that was all. If he fancied me he would have made a move long before now; he was never backward in coming forward. Roger quoted instances. I was surprised to learn that they had, briefly, been lovers. 'Paul . . . I can't give you any advice. You know the score as well as anyone. . . Just play it by ear. As usual!'

'How are things between him and Don?'

'Ending. I told Andy that you can't force a relationship to work. If it's going to break up, it's going to break up. He says that when it does, he'll play the scene for a while. Why not, at his age?'

I was disappointed, ready to put him out of my mind. Roger was probably right: but it was obvious that Andy didn't confide in him as much as I had thought; and that, I felt, was a pity. Andy didn't know me very well: didn't know me at all, in fact. He needed to if he was contemplating more than a one-night stand, as much as I needed to know him. Roger was clearly the person to ask, and he hadn't been asked. What did it imply? That Andy wasn't serious, as Roger had said? Was just playing games?

Later that day I was on the phone to Mick, my closest friend. 'I'm going out on Wednesday with a rather beautiful blond,' I said.

'Oh-ho! Tell me more.'

'A man, of course.'

'I didn't think for one moment it was a woman.'

'There's no more to tell. It will come to nothing.'

I'd convinced myself that that was the truth, and I didn't feel desperately unhappy about it. Life wasn't too bad: Rolf was coming soon for a fortnight's holiday.

I called for Andy at his flat. He was dressed in white trousers and an expensive-looking shirt: I became aware, for the first time, that he had really good taste in clothes. And spent quite a lot of money on them.

'What is that delicious smell?' I asked.

'My aftershave?'

'Yes.'

'Give-enchy.'

The flat was one large room, more pleasant than I had imagined, his possessions – too many for the space – in a sort of tidy clutter. Prints of Salvador Dali paintings, prints of photos of tigers, the Ants' Adam on the ceiling above his bed. Several flourishing house-plants. A whole surface covered with aftershaves, shampoos, deodorants, splash-ons. One bottle was out of place: Johnson's baby oil. A very good hi-fi system and a huge stack of records. More money here, I thought, than I'd expected. What *had* I expected? Or feared? Spartan bareness, maybe, or student-type squalor. Perhaps this guy, I said to myself, is not just a pretty face and an amiable personality.

I didn't really know where I wanted to take him, but the car seemed to drive itself back in the direction of my house. (I live in a village about twelve miles west of Exeter.) Not the local pub, I decided, pleasant though it is: I knew too many people in there. The King's Arms at Tedburn St. Mary was where we ended up. It *is* coming to nothing, I thought. Conversation was difficult, stilted: I was tongue-tied, and Andy, too, was more taciturn than usual.

We talked about Don, who was coming to stay the weekend after next. 'I haven't seen him for nearly a month,' Andy said. 'And I'm not looking forward to it, either.'

'You can't force a relationship to work. If it's going to break up, it's going to break up.'

He stared at me, surprised. 'Roger said that. Only the other day.' Yes. 'I shall tell Don it's finished.'

'Will you?' Now I looked surprised.

'I've been thinking about you, oh . . . all the time since you said you'd like to pinch me from Don.'

' "There's food for thought" was your comment.'

'Hmmm. It certainly has been food for thought.'

'What do you mean?'

'I'd like to come and live with you.'

Amazement was only a small part of my reaction: panic, mostly. I was being offered on a plate something I wasn't even sure I wanted. I felt like running away, out of the pub into the calm spring night, and driving home alone. It was . . . too bizarre, somehow. Difficult enough to cope with reality; the unreal – or the surreal – was totally beyond me. The Dali prints came back to my mind.

'Why?' was all I could think of to say. 'Why . . . me?'

The eyes smiled for the first time that evening; up till now they'd been unsure, avoiding me. Inside that skin someone was beginning to relax. Yes, someone: I knew even less about him than I had thought.

'Because you asked,' he said.

'A lot of people might ask! You could have said no.'

'I could have.'

'Well. . . ?'

'Because we get along O.K. Because I feel you'd treat me right. Because I don't want a life of sleeping around. I want security.'

He got up and went to the loo. Security! If he didn't have that already, he'd have to go through the painful task of discovering that it wasn't an ingredient that I, or anyone else, could inject into him. It would be like the worst aspects of living with Chris all over again. For the second time that evening I wanted to run away. But . . .

130

Andy wasn't Chris; almost the opposite kind of person. There was something calculating about Andy; at least what he had been saying to me sounded like that. If, for days, he had been assessing the snags and advantages of leaving Don and coming to live with me, that showed a certain wariness: Chris was impulsive, a neurotic. Neurotic seemed a ridiculously inappropriate word to apply to Andy. Was he in love with me? Nothing had been said, by either of us. Was it all perhaps a grand gesture with which he wanted to stun the local gay scene? He wasn't that shallow, that careless of people's feelings. Was he? I came back to the word security. It didn't necessarily mean what I had thought. It was an unfortunate choice, maybe: he knew nothing of Chris-and-Paul. Security, I guessed, meant stability. Not quite the same ingredient.

When he came back from the loo, the eyes were dancing with excitement.

'Let's go to my place,' I said. 'It's not far from here.'

'So I imagined!' he replied, laughing. 'I can't *wait* to see it!'

He made little comment when I gave him the conducted tour, but he obviously liked it. He sprawled on the sofa and I kneeled in front of him, kissing, touching. His response was slow and somewhat passive. In bed he would want me to take the initiative, I thought; he wants to be screwed. How would I cope? Yes, I would enjoy it, even if my sex life was usually the other way round. More bothersome was the fact that I could never initiate, sexually, these days; it made me feel false: but, I told myself, it could work out, not perhaps on the first occasion – though nothing was impossible.

'I'm not staying with you tonight,' he said.

'Why?'

'I have to be up early for one thing. And . . . I don't understand it exactly; I've thought about it and I suppose there isn't any really good reason, but . . . I don't want to sleep with you until I move in. If I may move in, that is.' He looked at me, waiting for an answer, but I didn't know what to say. He said: 'I still feel bound to Don till I finish it.'

'O.K. . . . if that's what you want.'

131

'I have had sex with other people while I've been going out with him.' He sounded bitter. 'But only because *he* did. He started that. With you. . .' He shook his head. 'I feel it wouldn't be right.'

'You do . . . fancy me, though?'

He laughed. 'Nothing is impossible,' he said, as if he'd read my previous thoughts. Abba were singing quietly on the record player. '*Andante, andante*,' he sang with them. '*Oh please don't let me down*. A good album, this.'

'Are you hungry?'

'A bit.'

'What can I offer you? I've got some cheesecake. Made by my own fair hands.'

'I *adore* cheesecake!'

After we'd eaten, I said, 'I shan't be able to see much of you in the next fortnight. Tomorrow I'm going to London, en route for Nottingham. Work – a weekend course for teachers; it's too late to get out of it now. And on Sunday Rolf arrives; I'm picking him up at Heathrow and driving him back here. He's staying till May the first.'

'It's all right. I wouldn't want to move in before then, anyway. Don won't be down till Friday week, and I was going to ask you for a bit of freedom after that.'

'Oh?'

He smiled. 'To see a few people I wouldn't perhaps see when I'm living with you.'

My eyes, for once, probably gave away more than my words. 'I'm not the jealous, possessive type,' I said.

'I think you're a fantastic person,' he answered.

In London I stayed with Barry Thorne, the most eccentric of all my friends, but one of the most delightful: he and his equally eccentric lover, Matthew Faye, had recently split up, but that was part of their peculiar charm. For it was quite unlike other marital break-downs. 'Barry is grumpy in the mornings,' Matthew explained – he came with us to Heaven that evening – 'and I'm grumpy after dinner. So we felt we couldn't go on living with each other.' He had moved into a commune of Gucci socialists in Finsbury Park, but he saw Barry three times a week and they made passionate, ecstatic love. Much better sex, he said, than when they shared a flat. At Heaven I met an extremely attractive man, and we decided to spend the night together. Andy wants a few days' freedom, I told myself, so why on earth should I abandon such a pleasant proposition? But what would I do, I wondered, if this situation arose when he had moved in? If life with Andy was superb the question wouldn't be asked: I could be one hundred per cent faithful without any pangs of regret. I was with Chris, for years.

When I arrived in Nottingham, there was a message from Rolf. His aunt had died and he had to supervise the funeral arrangements. He wouldn't be coming to England till the following Sunday, and his fortnight's visit would therefore be curtailed to a week. The gods smile on lovers, I thought, as I suppressed feelings of guilt at my sudden elation: all next week I could see Andy. I phoned him, but he sounded less than enthusiastic. Oh well, I said to myself, he's at work; he doesn't like the job much at the moment, and a baker's shop is a rather public place to show your emotions. So, unexpectedly, on Sunday evening I was back at his flat. He was tired. He'd been to Bristol on Saturday night with his neighbour, Phil, and Sandy, a university student, new to the Exeter scene. They hadn't got home till half past five in the morning: probably all found men, I thought. I'd done the same at Heaven, so what did it matter? I, too, was tired after the long drive from Nottingham. We lay on the bed together for hours, arms round each other, talking desultorily, falling asleep, waking, smoking cigarettes, staring at Adam Ant on the ceiling. I felt totally at ease with him now.

In Nottingham I'd sent him a card I'd bought in Gay's the Word, and he was obviously very pleased: there it was, prominently displayed on the mantelpiece. During the next few days, and the time Rolf was with me, I sent him several more. They came to dominate the flat. The first was non-committal, with a joky message; on the second I wrote: *I want* – your naked body.
– no sugar in my coffee.

– your cigarettes when mine run out.

The third said *I'm afraid of*

– frightening you by being too impatient.
– you not finding me as sexually attractive as I find you.
– you thinking I'm too old.
– being used.
– being badly hurt.

On a fourth postcard was printed: *Too much of a good thing can be wonderful – Mae West*; and on the back I wrote, 'Andy, I think I love you.'

I'd blown it, I decided: revealed more than I should have and embarrassed him, opened up a situation he wouldn't want to deal with. I convinced myself that this had happened, and got rather depressed.

I told Mick what was going on. 'Have you asked yourself,' he said, 'if he has any faults?'

'Often. And I can't see any. Yet.'

Mick seemed to approve. Not that withholding his seal of consent would have made any difference: but he might have given me pause for reflection. He didn't. 'When Don's here on Friday and Saturday,' he said, 'keep out of their way. Don't go to the club or the Hope and Anchor.'

I hadn't blown it. Mae West was decorating the top of the bookcase; Andy's eyes looked as if they were saying, 'I think I love you too.'

I had misunderstood his plans for the weekend. He and Don were going to Torquay on the Friday night, I thought; so it was quite safe for me to go into the Hope. I was alarmed to find them in the pub. And bewildered, too; they were both fairly drunk, but all over each other: on a real high. Don ignored me. When Andy went out to the loo, I followed.

'We've split,' he said.

'But . . . you seem so together.'

'I think we've found a way of being friends. Which was never possible before.'

'What happened? Did you tell him?'

134

'No. As soon as he arrived he said he wanted to finish it. I've told him nothing about you. It wasn't necessary. But I will. We haven't really talked; we will later, I imagine.' He was in my arms, kissing me. 'So . . . I'm yours,' he said. 'But I'm terrified of sex with you! I don't know why. Not that I'd dump you if that didn't work out. I suppose . . . I still love Don.'

That all sounds extremely confused, I thought. But he's pissed.

THREE

Despite what had occurred, Don still intended to stay the whole weekend. Saturday they were going to Torquay with Phil and his lover Brian; the Hope, again, was for me the only choice. There was certainly no point now in venturing further afield. At closing time, happy, wide awake, and full of energy, I wanted the party mood to continue, but no one invited me back for coffee. The club: it didn't shut till two a.m. As the affair was over, I reasoned, my being there didn't matter; in any case I didn't have to inflict myself on them. I could dance and drink with other people. The car found itself climbing up Haldon and speeding along the Torquay road.

Don wasn't there. 'We had a row,' Andy explained, as we danced. 'I told him there was someone else, but I wouldn't say who. It didn't matter to him, surely! *He* had ended it. He got very angry and jealous. And went home to Plymouth. But . . . I wish you hadn't come here, all the same.'

'Why?'

'I'm so mixed up.'

'Are you? I thought you had it all worked out.'

'It's been . . . a weird weekend. Can I come over to your place tomorrow?'

'Yes. Rolf doesn't arrive till about ten in the evening.'

'There's so much to talk about! My mind is bursting.'

We rejoined Phil and Brian; they were talking to Clive Forbes. Clive began to make a great play for Andy, who responded flirtatiously.

'He's been after me for months,' Andy said, when we were on our own. 'Nobody of any importance.'

'I've already told you I'm not the jealous type.'

Later they danced, like lovers (or, at least, a sudden exciting pick-up) and talked for a long while. It was nearly two: there weren't many people left in the club now.

'I wish you hadn't come here,' Andy said to me again. 'I'm . . . going home with Clive. I did say to you . . . that I wanted a week's freedom.'

Clive Forbes was no threat to me. He'd slept with Chris once, and had very little to offer, I seem to remember from what I was told afterwards.

'I didn't come here with you,' I said. 'So I don't expect you to come back with me. I don't own you, and I'll never pretend I do. I'm not going to tie you to a post. Go on . . . have a good time.'

He looked at me thoughtfully. 'I'd have left you for less. You're a fantastic person.'

'We haven't even started yet.'

'Paul . . . I want to make you happy.' He kissed me. 'The happiest you've been.'

The night Chris spent with Clive Forbes I had almost no sleep: tense, jealous, sick. That wouldn't happen now; I'd been knocked about too much since then, learned enough not to be bothered by such pinpricks. Andy would arrive at the house tomorrow afternoon; I believed that. He was, despite the muddle of his thinking and feeling, honest.

He was later than I thought he would be; not on the phone, so I rang Phil, who looked out of his window and said, 'The car's not there, but I think he's only just left. He brought Clive back last night; I guess he's taking him home now.' Phil, it occurred to me, would not have said this if he knew about me and Andy. Andy hadn't spoken to anyone, asked anyone's advice.

He was more than cheerful: radiant. 'The fog has lifted,' he said. 'I know what I'm doing. And I'm happy. I'm sorry

I'm so late, but I've been to Teignmouth to see my mother.'
No mention of Clive staying till early afternoon, and I said
nothing of what Phil had told me.

'Your mind's no longer bursting? And there isn't a great
deal to talk about?'

'No.' The eyes showed only contentment. 'Nothing of
any particular importance.'

I'd try to see him during the week, I said, but it
would be difficult with Rolf here. Rolf was flying back to
Copenhagen on Sunday morning; presumably he would
be leaving Exeter on Saturday night. Saturday, Andy said,
he was going to Bristol again: he wouldn't be home till
breakfast-time. He'd come over on Sunday afternoon with
as many of his possessions as he could cram into his car.
We discussed how we'd rearrange all the furniture, where
his pictures would go, his record player, the plants. I was
looking forward to it immensely – losing the stamp of
myself on every piece of the house, merging it with the
imprint of somebody else.

The week with Rolf was lengthy and very difficult.
Attentive, generous: presents – Danish pewter, boxes of
chocolates, goat's cheese, flowers – and my inner eye
and feelings were elsewhere. I decided not to tell him anything. It would have been too hurtful, particularly after
he'd come all that way, and a flight from Copenhagen to
London wasn't cheap. I didn't want to make him think
he'd wasted his money, nor did I want heavy, recrimi-
natory scenes. I would simply give him the best possible
time I could manage. He seemed to enjoy himself a great
deal; 'though he'd have to be extraordinarily insensitive
not to notice,' Andy said. It must have been obvious in
bed. Once I had quite enjoyed sex with Rolf; now it was
half-hearted, to put it mildly.

Fortunately I became ill; a bug that had recently
been doing the rounds, the symptoms of which were a
temperature, a sore throat, and a splitting headache. It
was a good cover for my problems, and Rolf accepted
it as the entire reason for my being off form. We went
out most evenings, exploring bits of Devon he had not

visited. Lush green countryside and ancient village pubs. He wasn't fooled, of course. He said nothing, but his letters after he'd returned to Denmark showed that he knew something was wrong. 'I was waiting for you to tell me,' he wrote. But I think I was right not to say anything, face to face. Mick says I should have told him beforehand and stopped him from coming at all. I'm sure that would have been too brutal, like being bashed over the head with a blunt instrument. Whatever I had done would have been hurtful: my task, as I saw it, was to handle things as gently as I could.

He knows the truth, now.

On the Friday evening we went to the Hope. Andy was there with Roger, but I neglected them until Rolf got deeply involved in a long conversation with someone about Danish dairy produce.

'You're giving us a wide berth tonight,' Roger said.

'I can't do anything else in the circumstances.' I turned to Andy. 'The record's in the car. Shall we go out and get it?'

'Yes.'

'It's yours, in exchange for a kiss.'

Cruisin' the Streets by the Boys Town Gang. Andy had said he wanted it, and as I did too, I'd bought it that afternoon. I'd phoned him at the shop, and said, 'I cruised the streets successfully.'

He laughed. 'I'm not sure I'll be moving in on Sunday if that's the case! What are you talking about?'

'The Boys Town record.'

I'd forgotten I'd parked my car right by the entrance to the pub, where straight people were drinking on the terrace. We can't kiss here, I thought. But we did, I on the back seat holding the record, he leaning in through the door. No one on the terrace was gay, and they must have noticed.

'You're in a good mood tonight,' I said, eventually.

'I've been smoking grass. And I'm tremendously happy!'

He arrived on Sunday, with his clothes and his perfumes, his records, books, jewellery, and his bathroom scales. 'Roger said what on earth are you taking that for!'

'Roger?'

'Yes. He called round just as I was leaving. I'd have been half an hour earlier if he hadn't.'

'What did he want? To see if you were really going through with it? Lots of last-minute fatherly advice?'

'Yes, all that. He's amazed. Amazed! And so's Phil. I told him last night, and he thinks I'm mad. He said why on earth do you want to end one affair only to plunge straight into another? Enjoy your freedom and play the scene!'

'Do any other people know?'

'Only Roger.'

'I've told Mick. No one else.'

'They'll all get an awful shock when we go to the disco on Tuesday!'

It was a good beginning, that afternoon and evening. One of my fears began to evaporate: what would we find in common; how would we be as friends? It was easy: our conversations were an exciting duet, and the silences warm and comfortable. We sorted out his possessions, rearranged things on the shelves and the window-sills, made room in the wardrobe for his clothes. The rest of his stuff we'd bring over the following Sunday – he intended to keep his flat for at least another week, just in case it all went wrong. We had dinner, ate our way through another cheesecake, and drank two bottles of wine.

And made love. Twice. It wasn't the most blissful experience I've ever had. There was too much tension and it was too . . . deliberate. Yet, naked, he was even more beautiful than I had dreamed. We had completely misread each other's preferences; he'd thought I would want to fuck him. Everyone makes that assumption: why is a mystery to me. I don't think the signals I give are all incredibly butch. Though why had I thought Andy wanted to be screwed? He was smaller than me, and therefore I tended to hold him in my arms: that was one reason; but more likely was that he seemed in no way to be an initiator. During the whole brief courtship it was he who had been the one who was chased.

It was certainly a happy discovery to know we had been wrong, but there still were difficulties. On each occasion – and I suppose, altogether, we made love about eight times the few days he lived here – I took ages to come, achieving orgasm long after him. Nerves, and wanting too much that it should be perfect, not being sure of how to deal with what I thought was his passivity (which later I realised was something else), worry that he wasn't really enjoying it: these considerations were the cause of my slowness, so that each session for me was something less than paradise. He doesn't actually fancy me much was an inevitable thought, dismissed always by he must do or he wouldn't be here.

He wasn't too inhibited to talk about what he wanted in bed. And he liked to discuss the men he fancied; extremely macho types in leather with muscles and moustaches. But, I thought, they'll probably, most of them, want to screw you. Yes, I know that the butchest costumes often harbour a lady, and a camp one at that, but the examples he quoted, whose sexual preferences I knew, would not have wanted Andy to fuck them. Here was another area of muddle: perhaps he really wanted to be screwed, and, like some others, was so frightened of the idea (pain, or the lack of masculinity it implied) that he had completely hidden it from himself.

I don't know whether he would have stayed longer if I'd been more confident with him, or if we'd done it all in some other way. I think what was wrong, sexually, between us was that he fancied me until we actually went to bed for the first time: the reality was a disappointment. He denied this, however, quite vehemently when I asked him. My blond hair is thinning and I'm not as slim as I used to be; but these are not reasons why sex shouldn't work, not the inevitable cause of a relationship breaking down. The fact that sex never worked properly was a symptom, not a cause, the most obvious indicator to both of us that the affair should never have been contemplated right from the start. An indicator we should have looked to long before he moved in.

He didn't love me though he very much wanted to; that was the answer. Two people who aren't in love can have superb sex, but when one is in love and the other is not, the parties concerned are looking for different things, and they end up with nothing.

But sleeping together was one of the pleasures of living with him that I miss most of all. I hate the other half of my bed when it is empty. My beautiful Victorian brass bed! He always slept profoundly, even if he occasionally travelled in his slumbers or talked – on one occasion I was disturbed by noises like a dog growling, but he had no memory of his dream when I asked him in the morning – and he wanted my arms round him all night. Some people, regardless of whether they're lovers or casual pick-ups, you can share a bed with and some you can't. Andy was certainly someone to sleep *with*; one of the nicest who's ever shared my bed.

FOUR

He was overworked and tired, but we enjoyed that first week, despite the sexual problems. His day at the shop was long. He got up at half past six, left the house at seven, and did not come back till six in the evening. With only Sundays free; he had to work on his day off because his boss was on holiday. My timetable had to be adjusted to suit his: midnight or one a.m. were my usual hours for going to bed, waking at eight. Now I was often in bed at ten in the evening, and I'd get up when he did. I was surprised that my body clock made no objection to the change, indeed welcomed it.

He was certainly half asleep that first Monday. A gentle, soothing time, necessary perhaps after the alcohol and the excitement of the day before. 'What are you doing for Christmas?' he asked.

141

'Christmas! That's more than half a year away!'

'I don't want to go to my mother's. I'd like to be here.' He looked round the room. 'It's perfect for a party! We could invite all our friends for Christmas night. What do you think?'

'I've not often had a really gay Christmas. We always seem to lose out, everyone obliged to return to their families.'

'We could move the furniture back. Bottles and food in the kitchen.'

'If anyone really wants to eat on Christmas night! You . . . seem to have it all planned.'

'I've been thinking about it.' He smiled. 'I'd like to ask Ian and Tom from Bournemouth to stay.'

'I haven't met them. I think. I know lots of people in Bournemouth, so I may have come across them at the Apollo Club. Would I get on with them?'

'Yes. Definitely.'

'A Christmas tree. I didn't have one last year, being on my own. I'll put a photograph of you on top.'

'Why?'

'I don't have a fairy doll.'

'Ha-ha.'

'What are we going to eat for Christmas?'

'Turkey. Then roast beef on Boxing Day. I've worked that out too!' The eyes laughed and danced.

I loved the reassurances such conversations gave. He was obviously thinking of being with me for a long time, though men of his age don't usually stay in one place. Don't usually stay with one person for more than a few months. If he was with me for a year I'd consider that a period of my life well spent. This would involve certain changes to the future I'd contemplated since Chris left. My summer in New York was the last time I'd been really happy till now; I was considering settling there for good.

'I'd better cancel that idea,' I said.

'I wouldn't exactly be happy if you went,' he answered.

We discussed the possibility of both of us going. He couldn't imagine anything he'd like more, he said; but we knew, even while saying it, that it was out of the question.

I had the offer of a job to go to, but he wouldn't get into the United States with no work permit, no employment arranged beforehand.

Just as well, as things turned out, that I didn't act too hastily.

But there were more immediate plans, exciting ones; a weekend – absurdly expensive, but worth it – in Paris, to celebrate. Andy had never flown before nor been to France. I went into a travel agent's in Exeter and booked the flight; that particular day I arrived home after he did, and tossed the plane tickets casually onto the sofa. 'Well, honey, we'll be in Paris on Saturday week.'

'You've *bought* them! Just like that, over the counter?'

'Yes.'

'It's incredible! *Saturday week!*'

Other conversations were full of looking forward to future pleasures. How he was going to stock up my freezer; in its entire existence it had been half-empty – I'd bought it for Chris-and-Paul, but Chris had left soon after: I don't think he opened it once, though it was he who had always said that we needed it – and now each evening Andy would return with something to put in it. I'm slowly eating my way through this food, and as I unwrap the bags there is always two of everything – chops, steak, pieces of liver – meals he'd thought of for both of us.

The cards I'd sent him he wanted to display somewhere in the house. In the bedroom, I hoped; they were embarrassingly private for the lounge. I had sent him several since the time I thought I'd blown it with 'Andy, I think I love you,' and he was, apparently, very pleased with them and the messages they contained. Proud of them, almost. 'Touch me. I want to violate your space.' 'What happened? Where did we go right?' 'Sex *is* dirty . . . if you're doing it properly.' And so on. I was wrong, I guess, in thinking they meant so much to him. He was flattered: probably nothing more than that. But it seemed different then.

And talking about where we'd put the rest of his furniture. What to do with his TV? 'Upstairs,' he said. 'So we can look at it in bed.'

'Yes. I'd already decided on that, too!'

I often saw us in my mind's eye, the pillows propped against the brass struts, he in my arms, both of us naked and warm under the quilt, watching a late-night film.

Small details of shared life to come: it would be all laughter, fun, excitement, happiness.

There was certainly laughter, fun, excitement, happiness, the short while it lasted. Disco night, for example. Gay social life in Exeter is pathetically inadequate, as it is in most British provincial cities. No club. One bar of a straight pub and the landlord despises us, though he's greedy for our money. A monthly disco: a jamboree that has to be held on a Tuesday, never a popular night as people have to work the next morning; weekends the management regard as impossible for us. Get more money out of the straights.

The pub is all right, I suppose. Dead during the week, but on Friday and Saturday it is often quite busy. Very few strangers, so it's not too good for cruising. It's just a place to meet your friends and talk and drink; perhaps, occasionally, to go on from to a party, or the club at Torquay. Or someone may ask a crowd back for coffee. If I had relied on the Hope and Anchor for sex since Chris left me I'd have gone demented with frustration. The disco, however, is always fun, partly because it *is* only once a month, which guarantees everybody turning up. Everybody? A hundred maybe; and fifty more who've strayed in from Plymouth or Taunton or other towns near-by where hardly anything happens – and the music is not bad, the drinks reasonably priced, and all one's friends are there. For cruising it's marginally better than the pub.

Exeter has one hundred thousand inhabitants. Which means there could be up to ten thousand gay men and women in the city. That figure, of course, includes children, married gays, bisexuals, those too old to want to be on the scene, etcetera; but where are all the rest? The University gaysoc is practically defunct. I know less than a dozen out gay students: in fact, I probably know *all* the out gay students. Roger says there must be another circuit about which we know nothing, but that's not true. The vast majority of Exeter's homosexuals remain in the closet. Not even in the cottages.

Exeter isn't London. But there must be enough of us to deserve more than twelve discos a year, and one bar of one pub with its smug slug of a landlord.

Andy's preparations for a disco were as tightly planned as a military manoeuvre – I had to bath and get myself more or less ready and have a meal cooked before he came home, so that he could devote the required time to his hair, his skin, his clothes, and his aftershaves. I fed him at intervals on chocolates; played Abba on the record player – *Dancing Queen*, I thought, would put us in the right mood for the evening – and ironed his shirt. I spent many hours that week washing and ironing. The linen basket was never empty. I wondered later if I did too much for him, and perhaps it annoyed him, was some indication that his independence was being undermined. I don't know.

The house was filled with the scent of Givenchy. And the result of his efforts was that he looked superb: in black leather, and wearing the studded arm-band I had bought in New York.

I wore my tightest jeans, and my new red and black striped sports shirt. This evening gay Exeter would see us as a couple: we'd stun them.

'How's it going? What's it like?' Roger asked when Andy was out of earshot. 'All honeymoon and lovey-dovey?'

'Couldn't be better,' I answered.

'I'm amazed! Particularly when I remember what I said in that phone call. I can't believe it!'

We told Martin and Graham, Roy, Charles and Trevor, Robin, Steve. Everybody. They hadn't heard; Roger – surprisingly – had for once kept his mouth shut. 'We'll have to put an announcement in *The Times*,' I said. 'So that it *will* spread around!'

'*Him* might be more to the point!' Andy replied.

'I love you,' I said.

'I think I'm going the same way myself.'

'Don't tell me until you mean it! So many of us speak too early.' I wondered afterwards why I'd said

145

that: why didn't I say, are you? And see what interesting answer he would give.

'At least I don't love Don any more.'

We didn't spend every minute together. He'd said beforehand that he would want to talk and dance with other people. I intended to do the same thing myself; disco night was our only big social occasion, and there were friends neither of us had seen since last time.

'I've got a new lover,' I said to Mark, teasingly.

'Who is it, Paul? Who is it?'

'You'll see him in a minute.'

'Is he here?'

'Yes.'

'Who is it? I *must* know!' Andy arrived from one of his little forays, smiling broadly. He leaned against me. 'I never guessed,' Mark said. 'Never!'

'Exeter's best kept secret.'

'But . . . what about Don?'

'Finished,' Andy said.

We drank quite a lot that evening. We'd been in the pub earlier, which I don't usually do on disco night: by one a.m. we'd both had more than enough. Friends said goodnight and wished us well, or told us we were crazy. 'Look after him properly,' Steve said to me. 'He's a great kid.'

It was pointless going back to my place when Andy had to be up at six thirty, so we stayed in his flat. 'I'm absolutely pissed,' he said when we were taking our clothes off. 'Glo-ri-ous-ly pissed! The room's spinning! If I don't sleep with the light on I shall be ill.' I didn't mind. I was ready to drop, and I knew that as soon as I touched the pillow I'd be dead to the world. 'I want to fuck you,' he whispered. I was very surprised: how could he want to, after all that drink and both of us so tired?

It was really good, better than yesterday, far better than Sunday.

FIVE

Quiet days, Wednesday and Thursday. Quiet Days at Clichy, I thought, remembering Henry Miller and looking forward to Paris. Porte de Clichy, Porte de Clignancourt, Porte des Lilas: the gate of lilacs. Paris with a lover!

'I'll have to take my watch to the jeweller's,' I said. 'It's gone wrong *again*! Third time since February.'

'If it still doesn't work properly when you get it back, I'll know what to buy you for Christmas.'

'A watch?'

Yet another little reassurance. There were dozens more. We needed a new cooker, I said; mine was old and two of the burners were beyond repair. Maybe I could buy one on H.P. 'Let's have one with a ceramic top,' he said.

'Expensive.'

'But ever so easy to clean. We'll . . . pay half each.'

Andy tired. Early nights, except Friday and Saturday. On Friday we met Martin and Graham in the Hope. 'You must come to dinner one evening,' Martin said. It was my turn to entertain them, in fact. Graham had been in hospital recently for a moderately serious operation, and I was feeling guilty because I hadn't been in to see him. I'd said to Andy, only the day before, that I ought to invite them for a meal.

'Come to our house,' Andy said. 'How about Wednesday?' I loved that "our".

'Who's cooking?' Graham asked.

'*I* am.'

'You'll be our first dinner guests,' I said.

We all smiled at each other. A nice moment.

Andy, at the club in Torquay, high on poppers, was a continual centre of attention. A solemn pale-faced man with a moustache kept trying to persuade him they should spend the night together; an attractive blond in white trousers passionately kissed him on the dance floor; Clive made signals; conversations started here, there, everywhere. 'Who are all these people?' I asked.

'I don't know,' he said, laughing.

'I've never been out with anybody whom so many men seem to want to take to bed!'

'Do you object?'

'No. It gave me a chance to flirt with Jamie.'

We'd gone down to Torquay with Phil and Brian. 'Cheesecake Lil of St. David's Hill,' I said. 'That's my nickname for Andy.'

'You mustn't mind him rushing about,' Phil replied. 'It doesn't mean anything. He's young.'

'It doesn't bother me at all. We came here together and I know we're going home together.'

'Lord! How I wish Brian was like *you*! He clings to me like a leech!'

'Phil . . . you don't have such a bad existence.'

'Ask him to dance, then I can go and talk to somebody else.'

But Andy returned, saying, 'I want this one with you, Paul.' The Three Degrees:

Are we in love or just friends?
Is it my beginning or is it the end?

'Interesting questions,' I murmured.

'To which you know the answers.'

'I do?'

'Don't stop loving me! It's . . . just . . . marvellous!'

When it finished I lifted him up. 'Little light-weight,' I said, holding him in the air. 'Nine stone nothing. You're a feather.'

I put him down, then he lifted me, effortlessly, walked across the room and dropped me gently on the carpet. Nobody came up to him now to kiss or to dance; they had all got the message: Andy might be an outrageous tease, but he wasn't available. Not now.

'I could go on till morning,' he said, when we left the club. 'I'm on such a high!' He jumped and danced and ran down the road. 'Why does everything have to shut so early in this bloody country? Roll on, Paris!'

But the moment I began to drive home he fell asleep.

148

Next day found us reading, of all things, *The News of the World*. 'There's a survey here,' he said, 'on what people do on Sunday mornings.'

'Oh? What do they do?'

'Eat, drink, and clean the car.'

'Boring.'

'And make love. Eighty per cent of them. Before breakfast, or after. Or both.'

'So . . . we're part of the great eighty per cent.'

'We haven't cleaned the car. Correction – cars. I'd forgotten we're a two-car family!'

'A two-house family as well. Have you thought any more about giving up the flat?'

'When I paid the rent yesterday, I was going to tell the landlord I wanted to leave at the end of the week. But he wasn't there. Which reminds me . . . the rest of my stuff: I don't think we've got enough time to move it out today. I must go to Teignmouth this afternoon and see my mother.'

News of the World Sunday morning. Afterwards, when we'd smoked the by now statutory cigarette, I was lying on my back, he kneeling, my legs between his. Both of us smiling. He touched my cock, cradled it in his hands. It was still semi-erect. He shook his head, eyes full of laughter.

'What?'

'Nothing.'

'Penny for your thoughts.'

'No.' Then he said, 'I envy you your flat stomach.'

'It's the way I'm lying. I can look pregnant.'

'I ought to lose half a stone.'

'Don't be ridiculous!'

'My stomach is not as flat as yours.' It looked perfect to me.

'You've been here a whole week. Are you happy?'

'Need you ask?'

On Monday making love was good too; except for the night of the disco he was much less passive than on any previous occasion. We are now just beginning to read each other's bodies correctly, I said to myself. But there was the same laughter in his eyes when he had come, the same shaking of the head. What is it? Though he wasn't laughing *at* me. Thinking of some encounter in the past? Don? Again, he would not say.

It was the last time we ever had sex.

He came home on Wednesday tired and silent. The usual routine with the bathroom: I had to finish with it before he got in from work. That, and cooking, and Martin and Graham due at seven thirty, seemed to account for his having little space for me, not even a pause for a smile. The arrangements were complicated by the fact that Graham didn't drive and Martin had lost his licence – the breathalyser had turned green, instantly – so I had to go into the city and fetch them. And take them back afterwards. However, despite the complicated timetable, the evening went off well. The meal was excellent – chicken, casseroled in cream and white wine with cucumbers; every bit as good, I thought, as Chris's chicken véronique, if not better: and certainly better than my offerings with Homepride cook-in-sauce. A crumble, pear and cherries, followed. Martin and Graham were on sparkling form – they frequently quarrelled in public, but tonight they were on their best behaviour. Andy was very quiet, but he looked exhausted. More than ready for our trip to France. When I returned from driving Martin and Graham to Exeter, he was in bed and fast asleep. Not a word, a kiss, a touch, produced any reaction.

We were to fly to Paris at twenty to seven on Saturday morning. This obviously meant that Friday night would have to be spent in London – Andy had got Saturday off work – and I had phoned Barry Thorne to ask if we could stay with him. He told me we could have his bed as he'd be out of town for the weekend. We'd leave for London when I came out of school at four. Andy said that he tended to take a great many things with him when he went on holiday. Half his wardrobe and nearly all the aftershaves; and was it likely that the hotel I'd booked would have an iron?

'I take the absolute minimum,' I answered, 'so it counts as hand-luggage on the plane. The most frustrating thing about flying is waiting for your cases at the airport when you arrive. You can stand around for hours!'

On Thursday morning, after he'd left for work, I sensed that something was not right. I usually had this vivid feeling, when he was out, of his presence in the house. Not just his possessions, or the scent of Givenchy, or the smell of him in the bed, used tissues on the carpet, a razor on the bathroom window-sill, the meat in the freezer, Diana Ross left overnight on the record player: something more indefinable, more powerful, had vanished. I went into all the rooms thinking, 'He's gone.' I'd had a curious idea at school on Monday – probably because I'd become involved with what I'd been teaching and hadn't thought about him for hours – that he wouldn't come home that evening, that our relationship didn't really exist; it was only a fantasy in my head. 'You are so ridiculous at times!' was his comment when I told him. This sensation, however, was quite different. I opened drawers, the wardrobe, to check. Most of his clothes had disappeared. And the cards I'd sent him. His sunray lamp. *All* the aftershaves. His iron.

He's gone. No doubt about it! For God's sake, *why*?

I found his flannel on the side of the bath.

True, he'd never said, 'I love you.' But I'd been lulled into imagining that didn't matter; there was so much else. He *did* love me: he hadn't said because he wasn't certain, one hundred per cent certain, but every other sign stated it loud and clear. The watch. *Our* house. The TV in the bedroom. Ian and Tom coming for Christmas. I'm yours. The new cooker: I'll pay half. Displaying the cards. You're a fantastic person.

It didn't make sense. Any way I read it.

I phoned him at the shop. 'Andy . . . what's wrong? Here, in the house. You aren't here any more. Are you . . . leaving me?'

'I'm not sure.' Long silence. 'We must talk. I wanted to, so much, last night. But there wasn't a chance with having to cook, and Martin and Graham there.'

'What's . . . happening?'

'Can you meet me after work? At the flat? At a quarter to six?'

'Yes.'

"I'm not sure." But *I* was: he'd gone.

Sneaky, taking all his things without telling me. Yesterday, presumably, he'd put them in his car when I was collecting Martin and Graham. Or when I was driving them home after dinner.

Have you asked yourself, Mick said, if he has any faults? Yes, Mick. I've found one now. He isn't as open as you or I would have been. The eyes are *not* honest.

I hadn't told Mick we were going to Paris. I'd wanted, childishly, to surprise him with the news at the last moment; I don't know why. Maybe to enjoy his reaction. Before I met Andy I phoned him.

His voice showed only pleasure that I was on top of the world. *'Paris!* Have fun! You sound really happy. I'm glad!'

Few other human beings know me as he does. There aren't many people to whom I've revealed so much. No one else can sense my moods so quickly, is so concerned for my well-being. I can deceive him, just like that. Can't he see the truth?

No.

One is always alone, utterly alone, at the depths of the interior.

SIX

Silence, while he brewed coffee.

'What's wrong?' I asked, nursing my cup. 'Is it something that can be repaired?' I knew it wasn't.

He shook his head and gazed down at the floor. Embarrassed, sweet, vulnerable. And very distressed. I wanted to hold him, say nothing had changed, there was no problem.

'You *know*, Paul. I don't have to tell you. There's
. . . there's not enough feeling. Eventually . . . I'd meet
another man. I'd hurt you more than I'm doing now.'

'Is it sex? I know it hasn't been that good. I thought,
well, it takes time, particularly when it isn't a casual
pick-up. I've . . . felt shy, so diffident –'

'It's nothing to do with you! Nothing! It's me.'

'I don't understand.'

'It was so flattering at first. Particularly after Don.
Someone who really cared. Then. . .'

'You found it . . . excessive?'

He nodded. 'Perhaps. A bit.'

'Have you got a handkerchief? I've left mine in the car.'
He gave me some tissues. 'I'm sorry,' I said. 'That doesn't
help.' Then he came over to me. 'Andy. . .'

He was nearly in tears himself. Again, I wanted to
comfort him, he was so upset; to say it's not important,
it doesn't matter. I remembered the card I'd written: I'm
afraid of frightening you by being too impatient, you not
finding me as sexually attractive as I find you, being badly
hurt. My instincts had been right.

'Is there somebody else?'

'Of course not!'

'Just as well I didn't cancel my American plans. There
is another life to put into action. I shan't throw myself in
the river; I'm not that sort of person. I'll sell up, emigrate;
this city has hurt me too much . . . Chris . . . now you.
I've exhausted the place. It's exhausted me. Andy . . . is
there any chance. . .'

'No.'

'When did you begin. . . ? You seemed to be absolutely
content.'

'I *was*! You said to me on Sunday – I'd been there a
week – was I really happy? That started me thinking. All
Monday and Tuesday, Wednesday . . . it was a lie . . . I
can't live with somebody I don't love.'

'Didn't you consider that before you moved in? You
must have thought, in those circumstances, it wouldn't
work.'

'I wanted it to work!' His voice was almost impassioned.

153

'I wanted it to work . . . so much!'

'Perhaps you didn't fancy me. Not enough.'

'I did. I did!'

'Then . . . when we actually got to bed. . .'

'No!'

'Should I have played it all differently?'

'You've done nothing wrong. It's me.'

'I hope we can still be friends. Go out together, enjoy ourselves.'

He gripped my arms and kissed me. 'Of course. I really want that. Paul . . . you're such a nice guy.'

'There've been quite a few people this year, since Chris left. And you're the only one I wanted. The only one.' A long silence. 'What are we going to do about Paris?'

'I don't think I should come. It would be awful . . . you'd be so depressed, and I. . .'

'But what do you *want* to do?'

He stared down at the floor. When he eventually looked up, he said, 'Of course I want to come! More than anything else in the world!'

'Well . . . I'm not going on my own. What on earth would be the point of wasting *two* plane tickets?'

Another very long silence. 'O.K.,' he said.

'I'll be off. I . . . need a drink. A double gin, at least.'

We met in the pub, hours later, and sat in a corner, talking. Our friends and acquaintances saw us, smiled, nodded, made no move to interrupt us: leave the new lovers alone. He asked me to stay with him that night, at the flat. I couldn't sleep. The single bed, my arms round him. Impossible! At a quarter past one I got up, dressed, left him a note to say I'd be back in the afternoon, then drove to my own house. And slept.

I had to admit to myself, grudgingly, that it did make sense. There was a kind of honesty in his behaviour from first to last, but a complete lack of thought. He'd hurried into it all without considering any of the implications. A rash, impulsive Arien, not the careful person he prided himself on being. He'd come far too quickly to live with me, and he'd left far too quickly. That was Mick's verdict when I told him. And Roger's. 'Done in excessive haste,' Roger said. 'You never bothered for one moment to find out beforehand what sort of people you really are.' I was just as guilty. The warning signs had been there from the start, and I'd chosen to ignore them. My haste was just as silly as his. Repent at leisure.

'The young are graceless and don't know how to behave,' Mick once said to me. Yes. Some of them. But Andy wasn't graceless. I was his age not so very long ago, acquiring experience and not knowing how to cope. Being loved can be worth more than all Arabia's oil, but one has the right to refuse such a gift for an almost infinite number of reasons. I had never pretended to reciprocate in order to exploit the giver for everything else he had to offer, as Chris had done towards the end. But I can remember trying, like Andy, to talk myself into loving. He had played at loving, had acted as the people in Hardy's poem who thought they'd go out to the barn on Christmas Eve to see if the oxen were kneeling: 'Hoping it might be so.'

'I can't forget Don,' he said, as we drove up to London. 'That Abba record . . . you didn't realise its significance. He used to say *Andante, Andante* should have been dedicated to me. It was our song, his and mine. It hurt, each time you played it.'

'Why on earth didn't you tell me?'

'Because you liked it.'

'You said the other day you didn't love Don any more.'

'Did I? I don't remember.'

'You said at the disco you were falling in love with me.'

'I don't remember that, either.'

'It all seems a great muddle.'

He hadn't left me because of a pop song. Or other minor irritations – he didn't much like my habit of leaving doors open in the house, or going into the bathroom when he was using it. Sex, as usual, was the obvious sign; more than that, the heart of the matter – as usual. The Clive Forbes episode, the refusal to sleep with me till he had moved in, the fact that he didn't on any occasion really enjoy it with me. I hadn't looked at

155

the obvious pitfalls: I was far too happy to find an end to my long loneliness.

I don't understand why some people say that sex, if everything else is fine, is of secondary importance. It's not only the start of it all; it's the *source* of it all: the sharing, the caring, the pleasures, the quarrels derive from it. Sex, in a love affair, isn't an occasional refreshing glass of water. It's the well-spring. If it isn't, one is better off living alone or with a friend.

It was not a time, however, to brood on suffering and self-pity. That, if it was going to occur, could wait till we were home again from Paris. There was every chance that we could have an extremely enjoyable weekend. Andy had said that he wanted the friendship between us to continue, and so did I. There was nothing that would stop it, unless I became depressed, reproachful, jealous. Friendship had blossomed naturally and with astonishing ease; there was no reason why we shouldn't go on seeing each other in the months to come. It was not like the break-up with Chris. I felt sure he would enjoy Paris, the whole ambiance: the beauty of the city, the food, the wine, the night-spots – everything. He didn't possess that awful facility Chris had for spoiling our pleasures. Chris always, without fail, ruined the high moments of life.

In London, an early night was obviously required. We were supposed to be at Heathrow at ten past six in the morning, which meant we had to get up at four thirty (not only to wash and eat, but drive to the airport, park the car, get from the car park to the terminal: all the usual delaying hassles of air travel), so we decided on one quick drink, then to bed. We went to the William the Fourth in Hampstead. I've been in this place many times over the years; and I've often thought that, unlike, say, the friendly bars of Amsterdam where you are instantly absorbed into a crowd, talking to two or three strangers before you've even struggled to the counter, here you could fall down dead and people would ignore you, probably trample right over your corpse. But tonight was different. I was with Andy, and his physical beauty was an immediate source of attention; also we were both full of laughter and energy. Energy is eternal delight. Bed at ten o'clock receded, and we stayed till closing time, drinking too much, as stranger after stranger came up to us. We could both have gone off with other men, I with Monty, an American from Minneapolis, and Andy with Neil, a South African from Durban. The four of us exchanged telephone numbers and addresses.

In the car, Andy screwed up the bit of paper with the South African's address and dropped it on the floor. 'I certainly shan't be seeing him,' he said. 'Not my type.'

'I didn't think he was. And I didn't like him much.'

'Your American was a bit camp.'

'Yes. But a nice person.'

'What was wrong with Neil?'

'He irritated me. He seemed . . . very persistent. What did you tell him about us?'

'That we had a relationship once.'

'I felt he was insensitive. To me. And rather wet.'

The South African probably didn't know that we had split up so recently, didn't realise that our trip to Paris had been meant to celebrate the beginning of a love affair; so maybe I over-reacted. It wasn't his fault that he was jarring nerves that were, to say the least, a little raw.

Midnight before we slept. When the alarm clock shrilled I felt stunned, hung over and only half alive. The last thing on earth I wanted to do was to get out of bed and put on my clothes.

SEVEN

The usual excitement and tension of airports – check-in, documents, the duty-free shop – made more pleasant by being with a friend (my last flight I was alone) and one who had never experienced the procedures before.

'Nervous?' I asked, as we took off.

'No. Nothing to it!'

In Paris it had been raining; the sky was overcast and the streets wet. But it was ten degrees warmer than London, where, despite a clear sky and a red dawn, the temperature was almost wintry. From the Porte Maillot to our hotel was only a brief walk, and, having dumped our luggage, we set off to enjoy ourselves, stopping at every baker's shop for Andy to examine brioches and baguettes; much more varied, interesting and imaginative, he said, than any English loaf. He was ready to be impressed by everything.

I had been to Paris last year; and two years ago with Chris – hot July days – memorable for many reasons, including the Bastille celebrations and finding ourselves eyeball to eyeball with President Giscard who was stuck in a traffic jam on the Champs Elysées. This morning the great arterial avenue was grey and damp, but just as beautiful as ever. The Arc de Triomphe and the streets radiating from it like the spokes of a wheel delighted Andy: it gave me pleasure to see his pleasure, to know it was I who was introducing him to the city. Lunchtime found us wandering in the markets near Les Halles, then over the Pont Neuf and into the lanes behind the Boulevard Saint Germain. Appreciating the quality of goods for sale, comparing prices in France and England in almost every establishment that dealt in men's clothes, jewellery, perfumes, records – and bread; gazing at the strange creations of pavement artists and street vendors, staring at cobbled courtyards and window shutters, tiny bistros and cafés. The smell that only a French city has: garlic and Gauloise. Andy's sense of wonder and almost child-like enthusiasm never flagged for an instant.

But our energies did. Lack of sleep caught up with us, and we returned to our hotel. In bed I was not permitted now to touch, caress, but I was too exhausted to worry about that. I woke before him, remembering the time Chris and I had been in this hotel. Making love with Chris in a bedroom in Paris – la vie en rose! How stupid to plan an encore with somebody else!

We ate that evening at a restaurant in the Boulevard Saint Michel, and paid much more than we had intended.

The wine was so good we had to have a second bottle; the sweets so tempting we had to try at least one though they were not on the fixed price menu: passion-fruit and raspberry gateau.

Yes, I said when he asked, I *was* being serious about selling up and going to America. 'And you? What now?'

'I don't know. I need a long hard think.'

'Try and get Don back?'

'That would be impossible! I don't know . . . I want a different job, and I want to move out of the flat.'

'New lives for the two of us.'

'Yes . . . and I've learned something.'

'What?'

'Never to live with a man I don't love.'

'I'm surprised you didn't realise the impossibility beforehand!'

'I just wanted it to work so much I assumed it would. I'm . . . sorry.'

'Don't be sorry. We have a good foundation for a good friendship. We bear each other no ill-will – no grudge, no blame.'

'I love being here, in Paris. With you. What sort of lesson . . . have you learned?'

'Me? Well . . . that I go on making the same sort of mistakes that I've made all my life. That experience gives me knowledge, but not wisdom: I can't convert that knowledge into action. I'll always rush impulsively into everything. I can sometimes be very patient: but my intellect never persuades me of the snags involved in what I want. Not exactly Taurus, is it?'

'No. More like Aries.' He was silent, then said, gently, 'I've hurt you.'

'Of course. But opened up many things . . . as you said, the pleasure of us being here.'

We smiled. And touched. I may have avoided touching him in bed, but that weekend we often kissed or put our arms round each other; moments of real warmth and affection.

We digested the meal by walking through the gay trolling-ground in the Jardin des Tuileries. Business was already brisk though the night was young; I remembered Phil so often saying, 'Don't forget it's the early bird.' Later, we climbed up the narrow winding streets from Pigalle to Montmartre. Paris at night, spread out below us; a hot night too, hot enough for tee-shirts and shorts.

In the Place du Tertre a street artist cut out our silhouettes from black paper. I have them still. Mine is the better; a good caricature, amusingly exaggerating the nose and the chin. Very recognizable. His is not right: it isn't Andy, and maybe I'm the only person who'd know who it was. It makes him look like Exeter's queen of queens, Lydia Boyles.

'Now for a gay club,' he said.

When we were planning the trip he'd told me he simply wanted to do the tourist things; he wasn't interested in exploring Parisian gay life. So I hadn't bothered to check anything out, not even consulted the Spartacus guide. The only club I knew was the Manhattan – scene not long ago of a particularly gruesome murder – and I wasn't sure of its exact location. On the metro a leather guy sat opposite us; we hoped he was on his way there, but he got out at Les Halles and I knew it wasn't in that area. We found it eventually. I don't like it much. It's cruisy, but it isn't welcoming; quite unlike any English gay club: no crowds of friends who may just want to talk and drink. In the Manhattan every man seems depressingly alone. But the music is good, and we danced until we were soaked with sweat. My jeans, once again, were plastered to my legs. *Cruisin' the Streets*: I peeled off my shirt. Chris had done the same that hot Bastille night. 'J'aime ta sueur,' I'd said, rubbing my hands in it. 'J'adore ça.'

Andy, feeling his lack of French made it impossible to indulge in his usual flirtatious expeditions, stayed with me all the time. He wasn't, in fact, as helpless with the language as he'd feared; he'd learned it at school and he was gradually remembering it. So much so, that when we returned to England, he spoke in French at the airport and in his shop, then giggled with embarrassment when people stared at him.

160

We'd missed the last metro. A long, long walk across Paris, Andy limping badly. We blew kisses at the gendarmes guarding the Elysée Palace. Bed at three a.m. And Sunday morning soon gone with sleeping late and being very slow with baths and breakfast. Montmartre at lunchtime, to show him what it looked like in daylight.

Sunday afternoon. 'I want to go to the sauna,' I said.

'What for?'

'Sex.'

He looked surprised. 'There's so much else to do I hadn't thought about that.'

'I had.'

'Hmmm. Perhaps your sex drive is higher than mine.'

I laughed. 'You haven't been roused by sharing your bed with a man you've been dying to make love with.'

'True.'

'Do you want to come with me?'

'I don't know . . . I've never been to a sauna.'

'The Continentale is the best in Europe. The only one Spartacus gives a five-star rating. I can assure you it's worth it!'

He thought for a while, then said, 'All right. Anything for a new experience!'

I'd been there last year with Barry Thorne. He had met Chris, by chance, and Chris had told him of the breakup. 'How is Paul?' Barry asked. 'Oh, fine. Fine!' Chris answered. Thinking this unlikely in the circumstances, Barry phoned me and suggested a weekend in Paris, the main purpose of which was to go to the Continentale. So much concentrated poking and pulling – the year, I must emphasise, was 1980: pre-AIDS – and heaving and prodding I'd never experienced, but the Continentale left me feeling depressed for a month. True, the sex was great, and why else go to a sauna? But I'd have enjoyed it more if the bodies had *not* been so attractive – I wanted to meet these people again, and not in there – or if I'd had a lover to return to. The anonymity, the refusal to have anything to do with someone apart from sucking or fucking simply reinforced my loneliness.

161

However, at this moment, I was more than eager for it. It's Andy's fault, I said to myself; so, if he doesn't like it, well, that's too bad. He'll have learned something. He liked it very much as it happened, with a young Frenchman called Marc.

Andy and I had arranged to meet by the swimming pool; I was there twenty minutes before him, and I couldn't help feeling jealous as I thought of him screwing on one of those beds. We compared notes over a glass of wine. Marc had given him a number of useful addresses – discos, restaurants, bars; a full night lay ahead, it seemed.

'Did you enjoy it?' I asked.

'Of course!' He smiled. 'Though I was nervous to begin with.'

'But you soon got over that?'

'Yes. Gay Par-ee!'

Our first stop was le Palace, a disco in the Rue du Faubourg Montmartre, which functioned only on Sundays, from six in the evening till half past nine. If the Continentale with Barry Thorne had been the ultimate in orgiastic sex, then Le Palace with Andy was the ultimate in disco. We both agreed that we had never enjoyed such magnificent sound, lighting, music. It made Bangs utterly second-rate. We hardly bothered to pause for a drink; just danced, danced, danced.

'This is the life!' he shouted.

'Better than Exeter,' I yelled back. Or London. Paris; the beauty of the place: I remembered Notre Dame, last year, early morning fog dissolving; the narrow streets to the north of the Rue de Rivoli, unchanged – apart from the traffic – since Toulouse-Lautrec; the Impressionists in the Jeu de Paume; the great distance the eye can absorb from Étoile down the Champs Elysées to the Place de la Concorde and the Louvre. Gauloise and garlic.

We ate at a restaurant near the Opéra, again spending too much money. But worth it. Lisettes, chicken chasseur, more rich gateau, a bottle and a half of Pouilly Fuisse.

'We must look at the shops tomorrow,' Andy said. 'I want to buy some Christmas presents.'

'*Now*? It's May!'

'I've got two or three already.' He sighed. 'Every year there's more! Mum, Roger – because he always gives me something – Phil and Brian, and. . .' He reeled off a dozen names. Mine was not included. Last week, I said to myself, you were going to buy me a watch.

'What will you do for Christmas?' I asked.

'I don't know. Go and stay with Ian and Tom.'

'It would have been fun, that party we'd planned.' He looked embarrassed. 'Suppose,' I said, 'I'd played harder to get?'

'It might have prolonged it.' He thought for a moment. 'Perhaps.'

Le Club Sept. Very boring after Le Palace: it seemed like a gay disco of ten years back. I had to save Andy from a guy who appeared from nowhere, covered him with kisses and dragged him onto the dance floor. Then to a bar near Chatelet, cruisy and rough. The leather man we had seen on the metro arrived, recognized us, obviously fancied Andy, and started a conversation.

'Il est très mignon, ton copain,' he said to me. 'Vraiment chouette. Ton ami?'

'Oui.'

Andy loves Paris and Paris loves Andy.

'Tu as de la chance, toi.' He looked at me enviously, then said Andy would make a great hit in Buenos Aires. 'Je suis argentinien,' he explained.

'Don't cry for me, Argentina,' I said.

He laughed and kissed us both.

We stayed there for hours, drinking beer and sniffing poppers. The doorman, a huge Arab, told me they didn't shut till breakfast-time. I talked to a man who wanted to take me home, hang me in chains and whip me; his friend hoped Andy was into water sports. Another guy told me he disliked the English – 'ils sont froids' – and Andy, he said, wasn't at all good-looking. What was I doing with someone so unattractive? I was much the sexier. When I said my mother was Irish, he asked me to go downstairs and fuck him. There was a wild back room, a cellar, full of writhing naked bodies; we'd peeped in there soon after we

163

arrived. It stank of sperm, poppers, and armpits. The only sounds in there were the groans of second-rate orgasms.

At one o'clock in the morning two outrageous queens started a Zizi Jeanmaire act on the bar; a third, dressed in what looked like curtains and wearing a sheep's head, swung from a lampshade. The proprietor told him to stop; it would fuse the lights. He continued to swing and the record player stuttered, then went silent. The lampshade had collided with one of the loudspeakers, disconnecting a wire. Andy, the moment before, had joined the queens on the bar, so his dance was abruptly halted. *Cruisin' the Streets*, the third time that evening. Woken from his private ecstasy – hey there, all you hunky guys, dancing to the beat – he looked rather annoyed.

We went home, another long walk, Andy barefoot. His shoes hurt, he said: I was reminded of Estragon in *Waiting for Godot*. I'd make a good Vladimir, I thought. Kisses for Mitterrand's guardians. Bed at four a.m.

EIGHT

On Monday morning I phoned my school and said I was ill. The headmaster, having no idea that the call came from Paris, was sympathetic.

The shops and the Jeu de Paume were a better idea than teaching. But it was impossible to get Andy out of Galeries Lafayette, so we never made it to the Jeu de Paume. Not that I desperately wanted to go there for I'd been last year; but I was sorry he didn't see all those Monets, Manets, Cézannes, Sisleys and van Goghs. He likes painting, modern art in particular. But he prefers a good perfume shop. I couldn't, eventually, distinguish one scent from another; my nose became drunk with the aftershaves sprayed on our hands, the splash-ons splashed on our wrists. Lagerfeld, Gucci, Pierre Cardin, Chanel, Aramis, and, of course, Givenchy: we bought far more than our duty-free allowance, though I didn't realise that until we were landing at Heathrow; I was reading the in-flight magazine at the time, and saw, with horror, that between us we had about eight times the legal amount.

'Don't flap,' he said. 'They won't search us.'

'You don't know that for sure!'

They didn't search us. Just as well: when I totted up our bottles of wine and cigarettes, they, too, were well over the limit.

Nothing else of interest about our last day in Paris. Apart from the subject of perfumes, I remember only one of our conversations. We were lunching in a café near the Madeleine; I exchanged long glances with the attractive and obviously gay waiter. 'You see, you don't get them all,' I said to Andy.

He laughed. 'I never said I did! You imagine it. You . . . you don't do too badly for your age.'

'It surprises me . . . you've never asked me how old I am. Do you know?'

'No. I'm not obsessed by a man's age.'

People often say that, I thought, but, as he hasn't asked, perhaps he means it. Or . . . he is no more than superficially interested in me?

I was the first to see him, standing by the barrier at Heathrow. Neil, the South African we had met in the William the Fourth. What an odd coincidence was my reaction; is he catching a plane, or waiting for a friend?

'What are you doing here?' I asked.

'I've come to meet you,' he said, smiling at Andy, who looked somewhat uncomfortable.

I felt extremely irritated. 'We're going straight back to Exeter,' I informed him. 'We won't be there till two a.m. at the earliest. Andy has to be up at half past six.'

'I'll drive you over to your car.'

'All right,' I agreed, grudgingly. The quickest attempt I've ever seen to install oneself as the new lover: the smell of the old lover was still in the bed. The lack of sensitivity was positively indecent! Yes, Mick, the young can be graceless and not know how to behave.

'You're wasting your time,' I said to Neil as I put our luggage into the boot of his car.

'I've nothing better to do with it,' he answered.

At least they didn't kiss each other goodnight. After he'd gone Andy said, 'I don't remember telling him when the plane was supposed to land. In fact, I didn't even *know* when the plane was supposed to land.'

'Yes. You never asked me. I had both the tickets on Friday; I'm sure you didn't look at them to check.'

'Do you think he's been there the whole evening? Waiting for every single plane?'

'Could be. In fact, must be!'

We both laughed; it was quite absurd. 'He annoyed you, didn't he?' Andy said.

'Yes.' I settled back in my seat; I was tired and wanted to doze. Andy was driving. 'Are you going to see him again?'

'I might.'

'Really?' I opened my eyes, and stared at him. 'You said you didn't fancy him.'

'There must be something interesting about a man who can do such an extraordinary thing. Waiting for hours and hours!'

Other faults, Mick: he's very susceptible to flattery. And devious. This meeting had been arranged in the William the Fourth.

I slept.

We stopped for a coffee at Leigh Delamere, and I took over the driving. I glanced at him from time to time as we sped along the motorway, and I remembered Chris on so many occasions sleeping beside me in the car, though Chris usually slept with his head on my lap – a sweet, intimate experience, despite the problems it caused with the gear-stick. And waking, to kiss and sometimes have sex. Nothing like that would happen now: I wanted to put my arms round Andy, pull him gently towards me, rest his head on my lap. But I didn't dare.

He stirred when we were nearly home. 'Hullo, Exeter,' he said sleepily, rubbing his eyes. Hullo, Exeter: that, too, reminded me of Chris – years and years ago when we were students – rousing himself from sleep and staring out of the window, dressed in a blanket. 'Good morning, world,' he had said.

'It was a fantastic weekend!' Andy said, when we were outside his flat unloading his things. 'Superb! All of it! I don't know how to thank you.'

'I couldn't have had a better time with anyone else.'

'Paul . . . you are such a nice guy!'

That's it, really. The end. He never shared my bed again, nor, I think, did we touch or kiss. But a long coda. During the next week or two we often saw each other. He came to the house to collect the rest of his property; I went to the flat with his clean washing. Dropped in to borrow a record, or lend him one of mine. After Paris, returning to work unsettled him. 'I really don't know what to do with myself,' he said one evening as we sat in my garden, drinking gin. The eyes looked perplexed. He was having arguments with his boss. He was going to move to a bigger flat. Or share with Mike from Taunton. Rent a three-room place at Duryard and live on his own. Move to Bristol. Nothing came of these ideas, and he eventually grew back into the dull routine of the shop, rearranged all his furniture, and seemed happy enough.

Did he miss my house, I wondered. I never asked. Just as I never voiced aloud other questions that came to my mind; would he like to return, live with me as a friend, sleep in the spare bedroom? The men he might bring home for sex would not diminish the pleasure his company would give me. Could the Christmas he planned be put into operation after all, Ian and Tom staying, the Christmas night party? But I didn't want to hear him say no; I was afraid of the rejection that would occur because I imagined we would not remain close. He assumed we *would* remain close; we'd see each other often, he said: go out for a drink, have dinner together. But I guessed he'd want to bury the episode in his past, not have me around, an awkward reminder. And how much, anyway, did he need *me*? Roger, Phil and Brian were his friends. 'I wish he wouldn't make such a big thing out of it,'

Andy said when Roger showed surprise and concern that we'd split up.

I saw less of him.

I was at Torquay one night, however, when he arrived with Phil and Brian and a fourth person, Julian. Andy introduced us, and it didn't take long for me to realise that Julian fancied me. 'I've seen you before,' he said. 'At the discos. And walking around Exeter in shorts.'

'I like wearing shorts. I'd wear them permanently if the climate was hotter.'

'Showing off your legs.'

'They look all right, do they?'

'Oh, yes!' He laughed. 'Have you seen *me* before?'

'Mmm . . . to be quite honest. . .'

At some point Andy must have realised that Julian and I would be going home together. I saw him looking at me; what did the eyes say? Were they wistful? Even a little jealous? I don't know. I couldn't read them any more.

Julian stayed the night. He was a pleasant, interesting person, and I enjoyed sex with him; I felt instinctively that he liked every moment of it, and that rather turned me on. We made no particular arrangement to meet again, but we said we'd probably see each other at the next disco.

A week later I found myself in a dilemma. I was going to a concert on the Friday evening given by the Bournemouth Symphony Orchestra in the Great Hall at the University. *The Unfinished Symphony*, Bartók's *The Miraculous Mandarin*, and the Elgar Cello Concerto played by the Bruce Forsyth of classical music, Paul Tortelier. As it would end at half past nine, the obvious place to go afterwards was the Hope and Anchor. I always do after a concert. But Chris was staying in Exeter all that week, at his parents' house, his lover with him. I hadn't seen them, and he hadn't been in touch. He'd phoned nearly everybody else, of course. Lydia Boyles said, 'I should avoid the Hope on Friday night if I were you.' Which told me that he knew they would be going there.

Well, perhaps I could manage that, but a further complication arose. Andy had invited a friend down for the weekend, and they, too, would be drinking in the Hope.

The friend was called Neil. He didn't tell me that it was the South African who'd met us at the airport, but I was sure it would be him. There were not, I felt, dozens of gay men called Neil among Andy's friends and acquaintances.

It seemed positively masochistic to force myself to endure both situations at once. I tried to persuade Robin, who came with me to the concert, to have a drink elsewhere, but he had to rush off and meet some friends who were going to a late-night film. I could go to the pub in Torquay, then on to the club, but I was intending to do that the following day. Fuck it! The Hope: it was *my* patch. Not Chris's any longer; he'd forfeited the right.

I took the precaution of having a couple of drinks in the Golden Lion first, for a bit of Dutch courage. Then went into the Hope. Standing at the bottom of the stairs – quite unavoidably – were Andy and Neil.

We talked for some time, amicably enough, about Paris. I noticed Chris with Lydia, and pointed him out to Andy, who gave him a long hard stare. I had, of course, told Andy a great deal about my years with Chris. They had never met, he said; I'd assumed that anyway, for he appeared on the Exeter scene after Chris had left for London.

Andy went to the bar. 'Are you surprised to see me?' Neil asked.

'Not at all,' I said. 'I expected it.'

Chris erupted into the conversation. 'Terribly sorry I haven't rung you this week,' he said. 'But you know how it is! I meant to, but there's so much to do and so many people to see. . .'

Don't give me this shit, I said to myself. It's insulting. If you want to phone somebody you do so. It only takes a few minutes.

'All my ex-lovers seem to be in here this evening,' I said.

'Oh, I'm just one among many now, am I?'

Did he imagine I'd shut myself up in a hermit's cell? However, I remained polite, though that was not easy; I gave him various pieces of news, such as deciding to sell the house and emigrate. Andy returned with the drinks, and I introduced him to Chris. 'We've met before,' Chris said.

'Yes, we have.' Andy's eyes moved from Chris to me, then back again. There was a long, embarrassed silence.

My brain whirled. When? Where? And on what terms? Had they fucked? In my bed, when I was in New York? Or in Chris's parents' house? Andy's flat? What did they find in each other? No. They'd met, but it didn't mean they'd spent the night – several nights? – together. Did it? Oh, what did it matter? I remembered a sentence I'd looked up that afternoon in *The Power and the Glory*, a sentence a colleague of mine and I had often laughed over, because it sounded as if Greene was parodying himself – 'It didn't matter so much after all: a little additional pain was hardly noticeable in the huge abandonment.' Now it didn't sound a bit like parody. Just true.

'You're wearing shorts,' Chris said.

'Paul always wears shorts,' Andy informed him.

'I know that!' He was a little irritated. I was amused: two men fencing over *me*.

At which point Julian arrived. My God, was I glad to see him!

NINE

'In the Hope and Anchor, I think,' Andy said. 'I really can't remember.' We were at Torquay; I had gone down there with Julian: Andy had turned up with Neil, Phil and Brian.

'When was it? Did he have his moustache then?'

'Yes. I didn't know who he was; I mean, I didn't know he was anything to do with you.'

Chris had grown his moustache after he had left me. So it wasn't in my bed when I was in New York; it wasn't in my house at all. Probably nothing happened: they had met in the pub, were introduced to each other by someone who knew them both (Martin or Graham, perhaps) and talked briefly. But it wasn't certain. Finding out would have been like the de Bono problem about the death chamber and the two guards: if I asked Chris he would lie; if I asked Andy he would tell the truth. Or the other way round. But I didn't want to ask either of them, so I dropped the subject.

I noticed that he didn't dance and flirt with other men now that he was with Neil. Nor did he seem to be particularly enjoying himself. He was unusually subdued: he looked at me once or twice with that same wistful or jealous expression I had seen last week. Again, I wasn't sure that it was wistful or jealous: perhaps I just wanted it to be.

At the disco two days later I spent the whole evening with Julian. Andy was with someone I hadn't seen before; we greeted each other, but that was virtually the whole of our conversation. At one point I overheard him trying to explain to Peter, who was going on holiday to France, the exact whereabouts of Le Palace.

'In the Rue du Faubourg Montmartre,' I said.

'How do *you* know?' Peter asked.

'I was there with him.' I hoped I sounded a little exasperated.

We went out together the following Saturday with Martin, Phil, Roger, and Neil to eat at a new restaurant. Andy seemed to object to my being there; the eyes showed nothing but annoyance and hostility. Maybe my asking him about Chris upset him, but I guess not. He didn't really want me as a friend; he had plenty of friends. I had, perhaps, nothing special to offer him, or seeing me apparently enjoying myself might have given him doubts that I'd ever loved him. 'So long as you stay friends,' people say when a relationship breaks up. 'That's the main thing.' It's extremely difficult. With Andy I wanted to, but it was he who was withdrawing.

Not because of Neil. That was no grand passion: I asked Phil how it was going between them, and he said, 'It isn't.' It was obvious anyway; I didn't have to ask. I felt sorry for Neil: he was as involved as I had been. I didn't care for him very much, however. He was wet. Insipid. Ready to please on every occasion, to laugh at jokes he clearly did not think funny. I mentioned all this to Martin, who agreed with me. 'Something totally unlikable about the guy,' he said. 'Can't even drive a car properly!'

So we went our separate ways.

It's very easy to fall in love and out of love. Not the same thing as *loving*. That's commitment, a promise you try to keep. Well . . . I find that to be so. You can't totally discard someone you really love, because you've given him something that is unique. The next lover is not a replacement; you give him a part of yourself that is quite different. But in most relationships there's a taker as well as a giver, a user and a used, a pebble and a clod. I think it may correspond with the fucker and the fucked. I'll always be the giver, the used, the clod, in every sense the fucked. Some people might imagine I like that, but it's not so: I want balance, and there has to be balance if a relationship is to work, and go on working, on and on working. If *you* are to go on and on working. Those who achieve such equilibrium are not thick on the ground. The taker, like a bee with the pollen in a flower, becomes satiated, and departs. The flower, of course, lets itself be used in that way; that can't be denied. The used is aware he is being used, permits it. And there are more bees than flowers.

The whole business of sex illustrates it admirably. Why do I like to be fucked? The opposite role makes me feel as if I'm pretending to be someone I'm not. As if I'm in drag. When I've been screwed really well there's an emotional satisfaction that screwing can never give. It comes from the knowledge that my lover is enjoying it enormously: my pleasure is seeing his pleasure. At its best I don't even need an orgasm. Feeling his cock inside me, watching his eyes as he comes, knowing I've given him precisely what he wanted or more: that's sexual satisfaction. It can stay with me for hours, even days. Screwing? Well, I've forgotten about it by next morning.

And maybe the perpetual screwer does forget about it by next morning. The way one has sex symbolises

– with more blinding clarity than anything else – the whole relationship. Affects the whole relationship. So – I guess – the taker can eventually become contemptuous of what is so freely offered, so often given; and what more contemptuous than to move on?

Am I polarising it far too much? Whatever our sexual roles, we're all takers and givers, aren't we? All pleasure is selfish.

'Our problem is that we're fascinated by the young,' Mick says. But I'm *not* particularly fascinated by the young! The unlined face isn't what attracts me, sexually. The emphasis on youth: something to do with the social structure of gay life as it is now. Where gay people meet – a pub, a club, a disco – most of the men are between eighteen and twenty-four. Where are the men of forty? Advertising in the personal columns of the gay papers? In the closet still? At home with their lovers glued to the goggle-box? At C.H.E. meetings, unhappily wondering what caused their sad condition? I don't know, but not so many of them go out drinking and dancing. Not in Exeter. I met gay men of forty – and fifty, sixty and seventy – in New York, and it wasn't in the bars or the wild back rooms. It was in their own houses at parties and dinner parties; and when they weren't entertaining, they stayed indoors with their lovers or went out together to the opera or the ball-game or the beach: 'I've lived with Bob for thirty-five years,' Jimmy said. 'I've lived in New York for thirty-five years! And I've never been in a gay bar in the whole of my life!'

In England, the gay revolution – the commercial side of it – came too late for the majority of those who are middle-aged. And why, if they're like Jimmy and Bob, would they even want to go to a disco? It would seem quite pointless.

So it's youth I meet. The bees. And always will if I stay here in this dull provincial backwater. I don't intend to. I'm off to America, to enjoy it while I have time to enjoy it. Not just for its suntanned fit bodies, but because there I may have more chance of finding the lover I want. I know it sounds like Chekhov: the three sisters who thought all their problems would disappear if they went to Moscow. You take your problems with you wherever you go. Particularly loneliness. But at least in New York there is likely to be more choice.

'You're wasting your time,' I'd said to Neil at the airport. I was right: he'll learn. That's why I feel sorry for him, and rather superior. 'Wet. Insipid. Ready to please on every occasion, to laugh at jokes he clearly does not think funny,' I wrote a few pages back. Rolf's letters have some of the same characteristics. We are all insipid to a lover who is cooling. Chris told me once, after he'd been to bed with another man when I – for some reason I now forget – was away, that he'd felt only contempt for me as he'd walked home. 'The silly old fool doesn't even know!' The cuckold is often a ridiculous figure. But when, in *his* absence, I went out on the hunt I never felt anything like that. Casual sex always made me want him more, and want him in a particularly gentle, loving, intimate way.

Andy, the story's finished. The idea of writing it occurred to me in Paris, in Galeries Lafayette, when you were sniffing Givenchy. This relationship, I decided, has something about it that's more like literature than life normally is – it has shape and structure, a beginning, a middle, and an end. Not the usual chaos.

As we dawdled along the Boulevard des Capucines I told him what I had in mind. 'It *would* make a very good story,' he said, laughing. 'What are you going to call it?'

'*Flux.*'

He thought for a moment, then said, 'An excellent title.'

'And I'll have every intention of publishing it, I warn you.'

'Why not? So long as you change the names.'

'Of course.'

'And don't talk about cock sizes.'

'Certainly not!'

'You can call me Andy. I've always liked that name.'

'Not Cheesecake Lil?'

'I'd sue you.'

On the last occasion he was at my house, I'd written chapter one; the manuscript was lying on the table and he picked it up. I could hardly snatch the pages out of his hands, but I squirmed with embarrassment while he read them.

'What do you think?'

'It's . . . very flattering.' The eyes sparkled – mischief, affection, warmth. And he smiled, that radiant smile I hadn't seen for weeks.

In fact, it doesn't have a very good ending. A beginning and a middle, yes; then it just peters out. I laid it aside and got on with other things. The new life in America needed my full attention: house selling to negotiate, so many letters to write, so much red tape to deal with.

One Sunday afternoon I was looking out of the window at the rain pouring down. Summer! What to do with myself in such weather? I hated being in the house: too many reminders – Chris had painted these walls; Chris's cigarette had burned a hole in that cushion; Chris had. . . A vase I'd bought him was still on the shelves. We'd made love on the carpet, just *there*. Perhaps, if I looked closely enough, I'd still see the stain. And in that chair Andy had liked to sit. I could picture him, in my mind's eye, bending down over the record player. This place is a mausoleum.

How was Chris able to move on so easily? I bought it because we *both* wanted it. How could he abandon, as carelessly as throwing his dirty knickers into the linen basket, a house on which he'd lavished so much care, time, affection? Because he'd paid for none of it, I suppose. Once it was an idyll, this house; its old beams, its log fires. And the ginger cat that disappeared for ever, a few weeks after Chris had gone.

There was a knock at the door. I was surprised: buried in the country, I hardly ever had an unexpected visitor.

Andy!

'What brings you out here? I haven't seen you for ages!'

The eyes were intense, the expression fierce. He seemed very nervous. 'I've come back,' he said.

'From where?'

'I've come back! To you! I've got all my things in the car, well, not all of them; I'll have to make another couple of trips at least. I've given up the flat; I've told the landlord. I've brought the stereo this time, and my pictures.' I stared at him, amazed. 'And the TV, so we can watch it in bed. You . . . always said you wanted to . . . watch it . . . in bed. . .'

'But the house is virtually sold. I'm going to America.'

'I know. I know! I'm coming with you.'

'I don't understand.'

'Paul, I love you.' Silence. 'Fuck it, I love you! I *love* you!'

Givenchy today, I said to myself as we looked at each other. It was a very long moment. Then we relaxed and smiled.